F
BLU

Blume, Judy.

Iggie's house.

$16.00

536433

DATE			

PRAIRIE SCHOOL – KILDEER DIST 96
1530 BRANDYWYN LANE
BUFFALO GROVE IL
60089
08/13/1999

IGGIE'S HOUSE

Also by Judy Blume

ARE YOU THERE GOD? IT'S ME, MARGARET.

THEN AGAIN, MAYBE I WON'T

IT'S NOT THE END OF THE WORLD

DEENIE

BLUBBER

IGGIE'S HOUSE
by Judy Blume

Simon & Schuster Books for Young Readers

SIMON & SCHUSTER BOOKS FOR YOUNG READERS
An imprint of Simon & Schuster Children's Publishing Division
1230 Avenue of the Americas
New York, New York 10020

Simon & Schuster Books for Young Readers is a trademark
of Simon & Schuster
Manufactured in the United States of America

20   19   18   17   16   15

The text of this book is set in 12 pt. Janson.
Library of Congress Catalog Card Number: 70-104340
ISBN 0-02-711040-0

For Lee Wyndham

chapter one

Winnie shoved a second piece of gum into her mouth. She crushed the wrapper in her fist and flicked it over her shoulder. A long low sigh escaped from somewhere inside her. She rested her elbows on the window sill and cupped her face in her hands. Kneeling in *one* position in front of *one* window for hours and hours wasn't easy. Especially on a hot and sticky August morning. But she hadn't moved. Not an inch! Except when her left foot fell asleep and she had to jump up and down to get rid of the prickly feeling.

Now her knees were sore. Winnie reached over to her rumpled bed—the same old bed she'd been sleeping in for the last eight of her eleven years—

grabbed the pillow and stuffed it under her legs. She chewed her gum as hard and fast as she could. It cracked better that way. Winnie was being disgusting —that's what her mother said about gum cracking. And this morning being disgusting helped her to feel less miserable. Earlier, she had slammed the bedroom door shut and hung out her BEWARE—PRIVATE sign.

The light rain had stopped and a breeze brushed against Winnie's cheek. It felt cool and refreshing. But even that didn't help ease the empty feeling. And staring down the block at Iggie's house didn't help either. Even though she could see only parts of it—the driveway, the gray stone chimney, a speck of the red front door. Just enough to remind Winnie that her best friend in the whole world was gone and wouldn't be back. There was nothing she could do about it. This was, without a doubt, the loneliest, saddest, most horrible week of her whole life!

Winnie heard a gentle tapping at her bedroom door. "What Mom?" she called, turning away from the window.

The door opened and her mother stood there, one hand on her hip. "Winifred Bates Barringer!"

Winnie cringed. Mom's voice got very loud. "Just look at this room. It's a mess."

Winnie agreed privately, but said nothing. She studied her mother, standing like a statue in the doorway. Mom was wearing her work clothes—an old blue denim skirt and a faded striped shirt with the sleeves rolled up. Her face was smudged with dirt.

Mrs. Barringer did not smile, but she softened her voice. "Winnie," she said, holding a tissue to her nose and sneezing. (Mom always sneezed a lot after she'd been gardening or cleaning the basement.) Mrs. Barringer blew her nose and continued. "You've been cooped up in this room all morning and I haven't said a word. Now, I know how you feel about Iggie moving away, but I certainly didn't expect you to mope around for a whole week. This is ridiculous! You haven't had a thing to eat today. At this rate you're going to fade away into nothing."

Winnie turned back to the window. "I'm not hungry and I'll clean up my room later. Okay?"

Her mother did not answer. Winnie sensed that she was standing there waiting for a better explanation. "I'm *busy* Mom. I'm watching for the new people. The moving trucks were here early this morning, but I haven't seen the new people anywhere."

"It's a wonder you can see ANYTHING with all that hair in your eyes," her mother answered. "You look like an overgrown sheep dog, Winnie. Why don't you try putting on some clothes and brushing your hair. It's after twelve already."

Winnie tossed her hair out of her face and

looked down at her pink night shirt. She cracked her gum louder.

"Winifred! That is DISGUSTING."

Winnie smiled. "It's sugarless gum Mom. No cavities!"

"I was talking about the noise, not the gum." Mrs. Barringer reached into the pocket of her skirt. "Here's a letter from your brother. As soon as I clean up I'm going down to fix lunch. I expect you to join me in ten minutes. And please Winnie, do SOMETHING about that hair."

Mrs. Barringer made a military turn and left the room. Winnie opened her brother's letter. But it was practically impossible to read Matthew's squiggly writing so she slipped the letter back into its envelope.

Matthew would be home from camp in a week and then summer would really be over. It felt funny to have a brother going into ninth grade. That was kind of old! Most kids Winnie knew couldn't stand their brothers and sisters, but she didn't mind Matthew. Not since last year when he started to talk to her as if she were a real person, instead of just a child. Which was more than she could say for her parents most of the time.

But Iggie's family, now that was a different story. At Iggie's house she hadn't been treated as a child. And she'd spent plenty of time there, too. She had slept over practically every Saturday night for two years. It was another world. Iggie's mother always put candles on the dinner table. She said Saturday was the most special night of the week. And she and Iggie were allowed to sample the wine. Winnie had pretended to like it but it tasted kind of bitter. After dinner they would move into the living room where Iggie's father lit a fire. She and Iggie would sit on the furry rug in front of the fireplace, then they would talk for hours and hours. Sometimes Iggie's mother would read to them. Other times there were guests for dinner.

Iggie's folks knew people from all over the world because they traveled so much. Iggie's father was always flying off to different countries on business. Winnie would listen to everything they had to say. Sometimes Iggie's father used to ask, "What do you think about that, Winnie?" Imagine! He actually wanted to hear her opinion. She found out not everybody thought the way the Barringer's did. There were plenty of other ideas floating around. And her folks didn't mind her spending so many nights away from home. Of course not! It left them free to go to the movies.

Winnie felt that she belonged at Iggie's house.

She wandered away from the window and over

to her dresser where she took out her freshly washed jeans. They were beginning to unravel at the edges where she had cut them off, but they still fit fine. She wondered if she was ever going to grow. She wanted to be tall like her father and curvy like her mother (although she wouldn't admit *that* to anyone). But so far, she wasn't much of either.

She pulled on her blue sweatshirt, regarded her hair in the mirror and stuck her tongue out at her reflection. She decided it was easier to hide all that thick hair inside her sailor hat than to brush it out. With a final check out the window she left her room and skipped down the stairs. She didn't realize she was barefooted until she reached the kitchen. The tile floor felt like ice cubes on the bottoms of her feet. She whirled around and ran back up the stairs, nearly knocking over her mother's prize plant at the top. She searched frantically for her new plaid sneakers. "Yick! They must be in the junk pile under the bed," she said to herself, giving up. She grabbed her loafers from the bookcase shelf instead, knocking over the giant copy of the world atlas in her hurry.

Winnie paused for a moment, but did not pick up the atlas. Was it only a week ago that she and Iggie had carefully measured the distance from New Jersey to Tokyo?

Racing down the stairs for the second time, Winnie smelled eggs. Her stomach rolled over noisily, but she had the feeling if she ate she'd get sick. "Just an apple for me Mom," she said.

"An apple is no lunch, Winnie. Or breakfast either," Mrs. Barringer said. "I'm making us some egg salad."

"I know Mom. It smells awful!" Her mother gave her a look but Winnie ignored it and hopped over to the refrigerator on the foot that already had a loafer on it. She selected an apple with no visible bruises and sat down before sliding the other foot into its shoe. "I'm going out Mom. I want to see what's going on. Maybe I'll go down to Iggie's house."

Mrs. Barringer turned away from the egg salad. "Winnie, the new people may be awfully busy today. I really don't think this is the time to meet them. Wait until tomorrow and I'll bake some brownies. Then you'll have an excuse to ring the bell and say hello."

"I only want to have a look, Mom. They won't even know I'm there." She was on her feet now, ready to move. "Bye," she called and dashed out the kitchen door before her mother could stop her.

Winnie stuffed her mouth with the apple. She felt like one of those fancy pigs in a delicatessen window, but she needed both hands to raise the heavy garage door to get her bike. She walked the red bike down the driveway, finished the apple and threw the core through the sewer grating. Then she rode eight houses down the block and stopped.

Iggie's house sat high on the curve of Grove Street. That was why Winnie was able to see it from her bedroom window. It was an old house—forty or fifty years old, Iggie had said. Winnie hadn't been near it all week. She was almost afraid to look up at it now. Her favorite house in the whole world. At least it had been for the three years that Iggie lived there. Winnie knew every little corner—from the attic down to the basement. And now strangers were coming to live in it. But it would still be Iggie's house. No matter what! It would *always* be Iggie's house.

Leaving her bike near the foot of Iggie's driveway, Winnie walked slowly toward the big, gray stone, two story house. The same potted geraniums that Iggie's mom cared for so lovingly were still on the front stoop. The bright red front door was closed. Winnie turned away from the house, holding back the tears in her eyes. An unfamiliar green station wagon rounded the corner of Grove Street and headed her way. Winnie ducked behind the evergreen bushes surrounding Iggie's house, just in case. She didn't think about the morning rain until it was too late. Her shoes sank into the wet ground and made a soft squishing sound. Her mom would have a few words to say about that!

She crouched and her heart started to beat faster and louder. Iggie hadn't told her anything about the people who bought her house. She said it would be a big surprise. Winnie didn't know what that meant.

The green station wagon rolled into Iggie's driveway. Winnie peeked out from between the bushes. The car stopped. The back door opened. Two boys and a girl jumped out and ran toward the house. Winnie's mouth fell open. She couldn't believe her eyes. In her excitement she leaned so far forward that she lost her balance and fell over into the mud. She covered her mouth with a muddy hand and kept her eyes on the new people. The mud was soaking through her jeans. She tried not to think about it. The three kids were followed by two grownups. Winnie guessed they were the parents. They were talking and laughing as they hurried toward the house.

As soon as the new people unlocked the red front door and stepped into Iggie's house, Winnie took off like a rocket. She didn't stop until she was almost home. Then she remembered her bike. She practically flew back to Iggie's, jumped on her bike and pedaled furiously down the block. She collapsed on the back stoop and yelled, "Mom . . . HEY MOM!"

Her mother rushed to the door, wiping her

hands on her apron. "My goodness Winnie, what happened to you? Are you all right?"

"Fine Mom, fine."

"But you're all covered with mud! Don't you dare come into the house like that."

Winnie shook her head impatiently. "Mom, never mind about the mud. I saw them, Mom. I saw the new people. And guess what Mom? They're Negro! All of them. The kids and the parents. The whole family's Negro!"

"Yes, I heard about that," Mrs. Barringer answered quietly, without smiling.

"Already?" Winnie asked, disappointed. "Who told you?"

"Mrs. Landon phoned just before you came home."

Winnie muttered, "She *would* know already. She always knows everything. Usually before it even happens."

"I don't like to hear you talking that way about a grownup, Winnie. Especially Mrs. Landon."

"Okay, okay." Winnie scratched her right leg. "Never mind Mrs. Landon. I should have known Iggie's family wouldn't sell their house to just anybody. I should have known it would be someone special."

Mom's face looked strange. She started to say something, then changed her mind. She brushed her hair away from her face and shrugged. "Frankly, I don't see anything to be so excited about, Winnie. Not anything at all." Mrs. Barringer stalked back to the kitchen and to the roast she was preparing for dinner.

Winnie sat there, still shaking her head and scratching her leg. Then she stood up and took a good look at her house. This was the only place she had ever lived. Right here . . . the same old house since the day she was born. She wished she could go *somewhere* or do *something* exciting. While Iggie's folks were discussing the world, her mom and dad were talking about who shopped in her father's hardware store and who did *what* on Grove Street. Yick!

Well, she was excited now, even if her mother wasn't. Maybe these new people were from Africa or someplace like that. Maybe they were world travelers too. Maybe they were like Iggie's family.

chapter two

Winnie's mom convinced her that a bath and shampoo before dinner would be a good idea. Once a week Mrs. Barringer insisted on supervising Winnie in the bathroom to make sure not an inch was neglected. Ears, nails and feet included. Winnie was not happy about having an audience. She especially hated having her hair rubbed dry with a towel. It gave her the feeling that her whole head might come off at any moment.

"Winnie, I want you to do me a big favor," Mrs. Barringer said.

"Can't hear when you're rubbing. Did you say something to me Mom?" Winnie asked, poking her face out from inside the huge towel.

"I said," her mother repeated in a much louder voice, "that I want you to do me a big favor and not mention the new neighbors to your father until after supper."

"But Mom," Winnie protested, "it's so exciting! Why can't I tell him before?"

"Now, Winnie. You know how Daddy is after a hard day at the store. He's all worn out. And surprises go over better on a full stomach. Okay?"

"If you say so Mom." Winnie glumly wondered if that meant both of her parents were going to be unenthusiastic about their new neighbors.

Mrs. Barringer brushed out Winnie's long hair and tied up with a ribbon. "You look so nice Winnie. I wish you'd wear it like this all the time. Nice and smooth."

Winnie glanced at herself in the mirror. "Yick! I look like Clarice Landon!"

After her mother left the bathroom Winnie put on fresh underwear and her white eyelet robe. She ran down the stairs to greet her father at the door. He twirled her around to get a better look. "Well, it's nice to see your face for a change, Winnie. I've been wondering what you look like lately." He kissed her on the top of her head. Winnie winced. Just because she'd had a bath and had a ribbon tied in her hair did not mean she was a different person. Un-

derneath the frilly bathrobe was the same old Winifred Bates Barringer!

Winnie ate heartily at dinner and smiled to herself all through the meal. She couldn't help the
growing excitement inside her. She was practically
bursting with the news she wanted to tell her father.
Finally, the bowl of chocolate pudding was emptied
and Mrs. Barringer nodded that now was the time to
let it all out. "I saw the new people today!" Winnie
announced. And when Dad looked puzzled, "The
ones who bought Iggie's house. They have three kids.
Two boys and a girl. I haven't met them yet but I
will . . . tomorrow."

"Well, that's nice Winnie." Mr. Barringer
pushed back his dining room chair and strolled into
the den. Winnie followed. She watched as her father
picked up his newspaper and adjusted the ballgame
on T.V. "Maybe now you won't miss Iggie quite so
much," he said, as he got comfortable in his favorite
chair.

"Oh Daddy," Winnie sighed. "This has nothing
to do with missing Iggie. I'll always miss Iggie. She'll
always be my best friend and favorite person in the
world."

Her father buried his nose in the paper. "Daddy,
I still didn't tell you the most exciting part about the
new people. They're Negro."

Her father looked up. "They're what?"

"Negro. You know, colored."

Mr. Barringer opened his mouth to say something, but was interrupted by a call from the kitchen. "Paul . . . garbage is ready!" He got up without his usual grumble and headed for the kitchen. Mr. Barringer referred to himself as the garbage man of Grove Street. He said he couldn't understand why his wife never took it out. It wasn't that heavy. But Mrs. Barringer maintained that putting out the garbage was a man's job. Same as mowing the lawn.

Winnie had no trouble making out the conversation in the kitchen, even though the door was closed.

"So that's why Iggie's family was so secretive about who bought their house. They didn't want any trouble around here before they moved away," Dad said.

"Some news, isn't it?" Mom asked, sarcastically. "Colored people on Grove Street!"

Winnie had heard enough. She ran upstairs and into her room, slamming the door behind her. She flopped down on the bed, then rolled over and stared up at the ceiling. Her parents never discussed important things with her. Anyway, there were no Negro families living in their end of town. And only a very few in the other end. So her folks had nothing to say on the subject. Besides, they liked to pretend everyone was just like they were. But Winnie read the papers and she had seen plenty on T.V. And just last spring her teacher had assigned the whole class to do a paper on "What I Can Do to Improve Racial Relationships." That was pretty funny, she had said to Iggie's family. What could she possibly do when she hardly knew anybody of another race?

Winnie closed her eyes and tried to think of all the Negro people she knew. There weren't many. None in her class. There was a kid in third grade but Winnie didn't know him. She knew Bert, the mailman. She knew Irma, who helped her mother spring clean every year. But she didn't know any Negro kids her own age.

Winnie jumped off her bed and sat down at her desk. She took a piece of new yellow stationery from the top drawer. She and Iggie had promised each other a letter a day, but she hadn't even mailed one yet. There hadn't been anything to say until now. Winnie took the cover off her ballpoint pen and wrote:

Dear Iggie,

How are you? I'm fine. I'm so excited about our new neighbors. You were right when you said it would be a big surprise. Was it ever!!! First thing tomorrow I'm going over to meet them. I can't wait!!! I'm going to do everything I can for them. I'm going

*to make sure they're really happy here. Remember
how your father said that people had a lot of waking
up to do? Well, I'm going to show them that some of
us are waked up already!!!*

She folded the letter in half and placed it inside
her dictionary. She'd finish it tomorrow.

She was out on her bike before ten the following
morning. She passed Iggie's house. The three kids
were on the front stoop. Winnie started to call to
them and then remembered her mother's brownies.
She rode home and came bursting through the back
door. "Mom . . . hey Mom!" she yelled.

"What is it Winnie? I'm upstairs."

"I forgot the brownies Mom."

"What brownies Winnie?"

"For the new people." Her mother didn't answer. "MOM," Winnie yelled louder. "DO YOU
HEAR ME?"

Mrs. Barringer came to the top of the stairs. "I
hear you Winnie. Stop shouting!"

"Well . . . where are they?"

"I uh . . . I didn't bake them Winnie. I forgot."

"Oh Mom! You promised!"

"Well, I just didn't have time Winifred. Now,
that is that!"

Winnie hopped on her bike. She wasn't going to

let her mother spoil her fun. She would meet them anyway. . . . She slowed down in front of Iggie's house and waved. They came down to the curb.

"Hi. I'm Winifred Barringer. But everyone calls me Winnie."

The middle-sized boy tapped the ground with a long stick. "You're a girl, right?" he asked in a gruff voice.

Winnie thought he must be crazy until she glanced down at her clothes. She supposed with the sailor hat on her head and the cut-off jeans she could be mistaken for a boy. But only from a distance! She took off the hat and her long hair spilled down over her shoulders. She grinned.

"I guess that answers your question, Herbie," the bigger boy said.

"Well," the little girl announced. "I'm glad you're a girl. I told them you were, when we saw you riding your bike before, but they didn't believe me. My name's Tina and I'm eight." Winnie nodded at her. There wasn't much to say to someone only eight years old.

"Actually," Winnie told all three of them, "I'm mostly a girl, but I can do some things like a boy. And sometimes I think like a boy too! Iggie told me that."

"What's an Iggie?" Herbie asked.

"Iggie's not a what . . . she's a who! And she happens to be my very best friend in the whole world. And this is her house," Winnie said, pointing. "I mean it *used* to be her house."

"This is the Garber house now," the biggest boy said dramatically. Then he laughed. "I'm Glenn Garber and this is my brother Herbie."

Winnie smiled at Herbie but he didn't say anything. He just kept tapping with his stick. The boys looked a lot alike except Glenn was taller, skinnier and had dimples. Winnie couldn't tell if Herbie had any because he didn't smile. And now he was chewing away on his left finger nails.

"Any boys around here in fifth grade?" Herbie mumbled, not taking his fingers out of his mouth. His voice sounded like a frog's.

"There's two on the block, but they're away for the summer," Winnie told him. "What grade are you in?" she asked Glenn.

"Sixth."

"No kidding! Me too. Maybe you'll be in my class."

Herbie took his fingers out of his mouth and did a little dance around Glenn. When he finished he said, "Man! How lucky can you get?"

"What's that supposed to mean?" Winnie asked, annoyed. He was probably a girl hater. She knew the

19

type all right! Always sarcastic to anybody who wasn't a boy. She gritted her teeth and reminded herself to be nice. It was important to make a good first impression. That's what her mother always said. She'd show the girl hater! She'd be polite and make conversation anyway. "Say Herbie! I see you've got braces on your teeth. My brother Matthew got his off right before he left for camp. I've got big front teeth. See. . . ." And she opened her mouth wide for their inspection. "My mom thought I needed braces but the dentist says there's nothing you can do about big teeth. When my face grows they'll look better. That's what the dentist says." Winnie stuffed two pieces of gum into her mouth. "Anyway, I like to chew and you can't do that with braces!"

"You talk a lot," Tina said.

Winnie shrugged and chewed fast. "Say! Do you guys play ball?"

"Sure," Glenn answered.

"Listen," Winnie announced, "we play in the park. It's only three blocks from here. There're plenty of kids . . . even fifth graders." She glanced sideways at Herbie. He half smiled and showed his braces.

"What about me?" Tina asked. "I don't play so good."

Winnie laughed. "Oh, they don't let girls play!

You can sit and watch. Say! Are you from Africa?"

Herbie turned away from Winnie, dropping his stick. He pounded his fist into his left hand and mumbled, "Man! Oh man!"

"What made you think we were from Africa?" Glenn asked.

"Man! I'll tell you what gave her that idea," Herbie said, facing Winnie. "It's because we're black! That's why. She probably thinks everybody with black skin comes from Africa. Man! I just knew this would happen."

"That is not why I asked," Winnie insisted. But she wondered why on earth she had asked in the first place. "I just figured that maybe Iggie's folks sold their house to people from another country. That's all."

"And you just happened to think of Africa!" Herbie said, accusingly.

"Look," Winnie explained. "Iggie's father travels all over the world and he has friends in lots of different countries . . . and that's all I meant." She hesitated before asking, "Where are you from anyway?"

"Detroit," Glenn said. "Did you ever hear of Detroit?"

"So now you think I'm a dope!" Winnie shouted. "Of course I know about Detroit. And I know about the riots too." There! That ought to show them she knew plenty! "Say, were you guys in any of the riots?"

"Are you kidding?" Glenn laughed. "Our mother wouldn't even let us out of the house. Anyway, we were pretty small then."

"How come you moved from Detroit to here?" Winnie asked.

"Our father got promoted and the company transferred him here. The company even found us this house. None of us saw it until we moved in," Glenn said.

"You're lucky. It's a nice house," Winnie told them. "Say! When you had those riots did your father . . . uh . . . did he take shoes?"

"What are you talking about now?" Glenn asked.

"Well, I saw it on T.V. and I remember that everyone was taking shoes out of store windows. You know, just smash the window and grab the shoes."

"Is that how your father gets shoes for you?" Herbie snapped his stick in two.

Winnie looked down and felt her face redden. She'd said the wrong thing again.

Herbie pretended to be talking to the sky. "I just knew she'd act like that. I could tell the minute I saw her."

This is awful, Winnie thought. Herbie didn't

like her. He *really* didn't. She decided to try a new approach. "You want to go to the park?" she asked.

"I do," Tina hollered, already running to the house. "I'll go ask Mom."

Herbie mumbled something to Winnie.

"What'd you say?" Winnie asked.

"I said we're getting a dog tonight," Herbie told her without expression. "A big, fluffy dog. That's the kind Mom wants."

At least he was speaking to her again. She'd be more careful this time. "We don't have a dog," she said. "I'd love to have one, but Matthew—he's my brother—has allergies. Dogs make him sneeze. But I get along with them just fine." Winnie smiled, sure that this time she hadn't said anything to offend Herbie.

Tina came flying back down the driveway. "We can go to the park after lunch," she said breathlessly.

"Great!" Winnie yelled, jumping on her bike. "I'll call for you after lunch and we'll ride over . . . okay?"

The Garbers looked at each other. "We don't have bikes," Glenn said. "We've always lived in the city where you rent them in the park. So we'll just walk."

Oh no, Winnie thought. *Here we go again!*

chapter three

After lunch Winnie made three trips to Iggie's house. One riding her bike. One riding Matthew's bike. And one pulling the red wagon she used to play with when when she was a little kid. She left the equipment in the driveway and sat at the curb. Now they'd have to see what a good neighbor she was.

"What's all that stuff for?" Glenn asked when the three of them finally came out of the house.

"Why walk, when you can ride?" Winnie answered with a smile, standing up. "You *can* ride a bike?"

"Yeah. We can ride," Herbie said.

"Well, this is my brother's bike," Winnie said,

hanging onto the big, blue one. "It's for Glenn to ride."

Glenn tried it out, making a few wobbly turns. Winnie breathed a sigh of relief.

"Now, for you two," Winnie began, turning to Herbie and Tina. "I figure Tina should ride in the wagon 'cause she's so little and Herbie . . ."

Herbie interrupted her. "Oh, that's just great. Everybody rides and Herbie pulls. Some fun!"

"You didn't let me finish, Herbie," Winnie hollered. "We'll take turns pulling the wagon. If you want, I'll start pulling and you can ride first." He sure is touchy, Winnie thought.

"No, no! I wouldn't want to spoil your plans. I'll pull first." Tina arranged herself in the wagon and Herbie pulled it.

"Follow me," Winnie called, jumping on her bike.

The daily softball game was already in progress when they got to the park. A group of girls sat in the shade of a clump of trees, to the side of the ball field. One of them looked over at Winnie and the Garbers and nudged the others. They all stared. Winnie waved at them and the girls waved back.

"Aren't there any black kids around here?" Tina asked.

"Oh sure there are!" Winnie lied. "Just not

today." She didn't know how she was going to get out of that one because when school started they'd find out the truth. But school was still two weeks away.

"Go on over there Tina," Glenn said. "Take your wagon and sit down by those girls."

"I don't want to." Tina shook her head and stamped her feet. "I want to stay here with you."

"I said *go on* Tina. Don't be a big baby." Glenn gave her a gentle shove.

"No!" Tina sniffled.

"Oh, for crying out loud!" Herbie said. "Come on . . . I'll take you over there."

Tina sat down in the wagon and Herbie pulled her toward the girls.

"Hey, Big Red!" Winnie called out.

"Hey, Winnie!" a tall and well built redheaded boy yelled back.

"Come here. I want you to meet somebody," Winnie shouted. While he was trotting from the ball field to where Winnie and Glenn stood, Winnie whispered, "I'm going to play a joke on Big Red. So just don't say anything, okay?"

Before Glenn could answer, Big Red was standing next to him.

Winnie said, "This is my new neighbor, Glenn Garber."

"You've got to be kidding," Big Red said, staring at Glenn.

"I'm not kidding! And he's from Africa too!" Winnie said. Glenn poked her in the back.

"Well, now," Big Red said, shaking hands with Glenn. "I sure do know a lot about Africa. I did a whole project on Africa last year. Took me a long time but I sure did learn a lot. Winnie was in my class. She heard me give my report. Got a good mark on it too. Right, Winnie?"

"Right, Big Red," Winnie said. Glenn made a face but didn't say anything.

"You speak English?" Big Red asked Glenn.

Herbie joined them as Glenn nodded to Big Red's question.

"She didn't cry," Herbie reported to Winnie and Glenn. "You'd think by now she'd stop acting like such a baby!"

"This is Herbie Garber," Winnie said to Big Red. "Glenn's brother."

"Sure would like you two guys to play on my team this afternoon. Would be a real pleasure. . . . Let's go Winnie," Big Red called out as he ran back to his position on the field.

"I thought you said girls don't play, they just watch," Herbie said.

"I'm an exception," Winnie bragged. "I told

you, I'm not really a girl. I told you I can do *some* things just like a boy!"

Winnie spoke softly to Glenn as they walked toward the field. Herbie ran ahead of them. "Big Red never lets new kids play. No matter what! That's just the way it is. He's really tough on new kids. And Herbie is . . . well . . . you know . . . well, I just didn't want him to get the wrong idea. So it's just a little joke on Big Red 'cause he thinks he knows so much!"

"You're a nut Winnie. A regular nut!" Glenn said.

Winnie figured that was a compliment.

One hot and sweaty hour later the game was over. Actually the game was *never* really over. It continued from day to day. Sometimes they didn't even keep score. Winnie was disappointed in Glenn and Herbie, but she tried not to show it. She thought they would be great athletes. But Glenn didn't play any better than she did. And she was a girl! Herbie ran fast but he dropped two fly balls in left field.

The rain that had cooled things off yesterday had given way to a bright sun beating down on their bare heads. Winnie put a rubber band around her hair to hold it on top of her head. It stood up like a big, floppy brush. She always wore the rubber band around her ankle, just in case she needed it. Her mother told her that was a very dangerous thing to do. It could stop all the blood from circulating and then she'd be dead! But Winnie didn't believe it.

They collected Tina and the wagon. As they were leaving the park grounds Glenn paused and called to Big Red. "Bye. Thanks for the game. Oh, by the way . . . we're really from Detroit. That's Michigan, *not* Africa!" Glenn and Winnie laughed as Big Red's mouth fell open. They didn't hang around long enough to give him a chance to reply. Winnie figured he'd be hopping mad for a few days, but he'd get over it.

On the way home they rode down Sherbrooke Road, where three new houses were going up. There was plenty of noise and lots of action, so they stopped to watch. Winnie spotted one workman up on the roof eating something. Maybe his lunch. He waved down at them and Winnie giggled. He looked like a monkey at the zoo, doing funny tricks. They stood there enjoying the show until one of the men told them to be on their way. He didn't want to be responsible for any accidents.

In fifteen minutes they were back on Grove Street. Little beads of perspiration stood out on all their faces, except Tina's. She was cool and content riding in the wagon.

Winnie was exhausted. That Herbie Garber was pretty smart to volunteer to pull the wagon on the way *to* the park. Why hadn't she thought of that!

Three houses before Iggie's Tina called out, "Stop!"

"What's the matter, Tina?" Winnie asked.

"Up there . . . on the porch," Tina pointed.

Winnie looked up and groaned. Clarice Landon was perched like a kitten in the corner of her front porch, playing with paper dolls. Usually she sat in a rocking chair, like a little old lady.

"Who's that?" Tina asked. "She's pretty."

Winnie whispered. "That's Clarice Landon and she's awful. So's her mother. I can't stand them."

Winnie was used to the way Clarice looked all right. Only she didn't call it pretty. *Immaculate!* Mrs. Barringer said. Naturally Clarice was always a big hit with mothers and teachers, in her starched dresses and ribboned hair. Yick!

Winnie started to pull the wagon again, but before she got past the Landon's house Clarice put down her paper dolls and skipped down the front walk.

"Hi, Winnie."

Winnie muttered, "Hi, Clarice. This is Glenn, Herbie and Tina. They just moved into Iggie's house."

"I know," Clarice said. "I know all about them from my mother." She grinned sheepishly at Winnie while stealing a glance at the Garbers.

Winnie couldn't help making a face at the mention of Mrs. Landon. There was something about that woman . . . something underneath the soft voice and sweet smile. Maybe it was that all the grownups on the block thought she was the greatest . . . including the Barringers! Winnie had heard her father say dozens of times: "Dorothy Landon is a sensible woman. She has a real head on her shoulders." And Mrs. Barringer agreed. "I don't know how she does it! All those meetings and still the best housekeeper I know." Yick! No matter what her parents thought, Winnie knew for sure that Mrs. Landon was an old busybody. Just last month her mother forced her to go to Clarice's birthday party (and in a new dress too!) Mrs. Landon had flashed her phony smile and said, "What a perfectly lovely dress, Winifred. It looks so expensive. Was it?" Now that was plain old "nosey." And there was that rainy day when Mrs. Landon had driven her home from the bus stop. "I saw so many cars at your house Saturday night, Winifred. Did your parents have a party?" And when Winnie told her, yes, they had, Mrs. Landon said, "How nice! Anyone there I know?" Well, that was "nosey" too! Even if Winnie's mom thought

Mrs. Landon was just being sociable and making conversation. Winnie knew better. And Mr. Landon! He was always saying: "Yes dear. Of *course* dear. Whatever you *say* dear." Yick! It was sickening. Princess Clarice was supposed to be on the lookout for germs all the time. She wasn't supposed to eat or drink anything at other people's houses. Oh, Winnie knew all about them all right! Little Miss Germ-Head and her mother, Germs, Incorporated!

But did Tina take her advice? No! She went right on talking to Clarice. "Want to come over to play?" Tina asked.

Clarice answered so softly no one understood her.

Tina continued. "It doesn't have to be today. How 'bout tomorrow?"

This time there was no mistaking Little Miss Germ-Head's reply. "My mother says I can't play with any colored kids." Clarice ran back up the front walk, to her rocking chair and paper dolls.

Winnie felt sick. How could anybody say a thing like that?

Herbie started up the Landon's walk. "Man! I ought to give that no good lousy little kid a . . ."

Glenn grabbed him by the sleeve. "Cut it out Herbie. Forget it."

"Sure . . . forget it! Just like that!" Herbie snapped his fingers."

"Well, I warned you about Little Miss Germ-Head."

"I don't have any germs," Tina whispered. "No germs at all."

"Everybody has germs," Herbie said.

"I don't!" Tina insisted.

"Sure you do," Glenn told her. "We all do. Even Miss Germ-Head has germs."

"*Especially* Miss Germ-Head!" Herbie agreed.

"No point in hanging around here," Winnie said. "Come on Tina . . . I'll pull you home."

The boys left the bikes in Iggie's driveway but Winnie pulled Tina all the way to the back of the house.

Herbie yelled through the screen door. "Hey Mom! How about some lemonade? We're beat!"

"Lemonade!" A voice shouted from inside the house. "I've got eight million things to do and you come home hollering for lemonade!"

Herbie flapped his arms and raised his eyes to the sky. Mrs. Garber came to the back door. She saw Winnie and laughed. "Oh, I didn't know you had company." She seemed embarrassed as she wiped her hands on her slacks.

"This is Winnie, Mom. From down the street," Glenn said.

"Hello Winnie." Her voice was gruff, like Herbie's. She had a pretty smile. "I'm, uh, sorry about the

33

lemonade." Winnie had the feeling the apology was for her benefit. "I'm just so busy trying to get unpacked. We do have some grape juice. Would you like some?"

"I'm really not too thirsty," Winnie lied. "I wouldn't want to put you to any trouble."

"It's no trouble. Tina will help me. Come on Tina."

Tina and her mother disappeared into the house. They came back with a big can of juice and some paper cups. Winnie gulped down two cups of grape juice and told Mrs. Garber that she had to be going, using what she considered her very best manners and most charming voice. She forgot to take home Matthew's bike and the red wagon. She rode home slowly wondering if Tina or the boys would tell their mother about Little Miss Germ-Head.

chapter four

After dinner Winnie sat in her room reading her letter to Iggie. It didn't sound right now that she'd met the Garbers. She ripped it up and threw the pieces into the waste basket. She took out a fresh piece of paper and began again.

Dear Iggie,

How are you? I'm fine. You wouldn't believe what happened here. First of all I met the Garbers (the people who bought your house) and they have three kids. Anyway, the day started out pretty good. I was really nice and friendly and took the new kids

*to the park but then on the way home who should we
bump into but Clarice and she had to open her fat
mouth and say how her mother (Good Old Germs)
said she can't play with any colored kids. Well, I'm
telling you I wanted to die. I mean, what could I say?
And anyway the Garbers don't even say colored . . .
they say black.*

Winnie heard the chime of the front doorbell.
She wrote "to be continued" and jumped up and
headed for the hall.

"I'll get it!" she hollered as she practically flew
down the stairs. She liked to be the first one to the
door and the phone. That irritated her father when
he was expecting a business call, but she kept on
doing it anyway. It was fun to be the first to know
what was going on. As soon as Winnie opened the
front door she was sorry she had been in such a hurry.
She stood face to face with Mrs. Dorothy Landon.
Germs, Incorporated!

"Good evening, Winifred. Are your parents at
home?" Mrs. Landon asked.

Winnie tried to concentrate on Mrs. Landon's
eyeglasses. They hung from a gold chain around her
neck, and rested a few inches below her chin. That
way Winnie could avoid looking directly at Mrs.
Landon's face. Germs, Incorporated only wore her

glasses on her eyes when she had to see something really important. Winnie sniffed. Mrs. Landon smelled like beauty parlor. Her usual sweater was thrown over her shoulders. She always wore one . . . even if it was boiling hot.

"I said, are your parents at home, Winifred?"

"Oh. Wait a second and I'll see," Winnie answered, knowing very well that her mom and dad were out on the back porch. She yelled as loud as she could (without turning away from Mrs. Landon). "MOM! DAD! . . . ANYBODY HOME?"

Mrs. Landon backed away from Winnie. "My, my," she said, talking through her teeth and turning on the smile. "Don't we have healthy lungs this evening."

Mr. Barringer walked in from the porch and Winnie raced up the stairs, with her tongue stuck out. No one noticed, but it made her feel better about being polite (well, almost polite) to Mrs. Landon.

At the top of the stairs Winnie crouched behind the big potted plant. She peeked out through the openings in the wooden bannister. She didn't want to miss a thing. Mrs. Landon never "just dropped in." There was *always* a reason.

Mrs. Barringer came in from the porch too. "Dorothy . . . hello. I haven't seen you in a while. How are you?"

"Yick!" Winnie whispered to herself.

"I'm upset, Helen," Mrs. Landon told Winnie's mother.

"Well, what can we do to help, Dorothy?" Mr. Barringer asked.

Mrs. Landon's smile disappeared and Winnie thought her face looked like she had just finished sucking a lemon.

"I have a petition with me, Paul. I hope that you and Helen will be sensible and sign it immediately. Every minute counts."

Winnie had to strain to hear. Mrs. Landon's voice was so low.

Mr. Barringer laughed good naturedly. "And what are we petitioning for *this* week, Dorothy?"

"I'm afraid it's rather unpleasant," Mrs. Landon answered. "But someone has to do something."

"About what, Dorothy?"

"About the Garber family."

"Oh," Mr. Barringer said. "I just don't know, Dorothy. I just don't know . . ." Mr. Barringer confessed.

Winnie whispered from the top of the stairs, "Tell her off, Daddy. Come on . . . tell her what she really is. . . ."

Mrs. Landon put on her glasses. "Look Paul, if we sit around and talk about it, nothing is going to be accomplished. What we need is a little action." She flashed the smile and her voice cooed. "Now, I have nothing against the Garbers personally. I just want our *lovely* neighborhood to stay the way it is. As I'm sure you do."

Winnie's dad coughed, but Mrs. Landon continued. "Face it Paul . . . things won't stay the same if the Garbers live here. You know as well as I what will happen to our schools . . . our community . . . to everything! Once *that* element takes over, forget it! We've got to act now."

"What do you have in mind, Dorothy?" Mr. Barringer asked.

"For a start . . . this petition. Let the Garbers know that they won't be happy here. People rarely stay where they aren't wanted."

Winnie groaned softly to herself. "Oh Daddy! Don't be nice to her. Please don't even let her think you might sign that thing. Please Daddy! *Please*."

"Of course I'll be pleasant about it," Mrs. Landon promised. "We don't want any headlines."

"Naturally!" Winnie practically spat. "Good old Germs! Always pleasant!"

"I see," Mr. Barringer said. "And if your petition doesn't work . . . then what?"

"Well . . ." Mrs. Landon tapped her petition with a red marking pen. "Then we'll have to put on the pressure, Paul. We'll have to let them know that we *really* mean business. I'm sure they'll understand."

"What does Fred think about all of this?" Mr. Barringer asked.

"Fred Landon is behind me one hundred per cent!"

Winnie muttered, "Yes dear. Of *course* dear. Whatever you *say* dear."

"Well, Dorothy . . . Helen and I haven't had a chance to talk this over yet. But I'll think about it. And I'll be in touch with you when I reach a decision."

Winnie whispered. "Tell her you'll never reach that kind of decision, Daddy. Go ahead and tell her."

Mrs. Landon carefully removed her glasses and let them hang around her neck again. "Fine Paul. I knew I could count on you and Helen. You're sensible people."

"We'll see, Dorothy," Mr. Barringer said, walking Mrs. Landon to the door. "Good night."

"Good night, Helen. Good night, Paul," Germs called.

Mr. Barringer closed the door quietly.

"Why didn't you sign it?" Mrs. Barringer asked angrily.

"I don't know if I want to," Mr. Barringer said.

"But there can't be any doubt, Paul. You *should* have signed it right away. Dorothy Landon always knows what she's talking about when it comes to community affairs."

"I'm not so sure," Mr. Barringer said.

"But Paul, you've always valued her opinion."

"I supported her when she fought for higher teachers' salaries, yes. I voted for her three times for the board of education, yes! But I'm not so sure about this. Everything she had to say was a lot of double talk."

"I got her point," Mrs. Barringer said.

"I'm sure you did, Helen."

"Well, I hope Winnie didn't hear anything. Children shouldn't have to know about these problems."

"Ha!" Winnie said as she crawled along the floor, back to her own room. Why didn't parents ever do what you wanted them to do? She felt like screaming, but then they would know she had been listening and she wasn't in the mood for a lecture. She took off her shoes and flung them across her room. Then she flopped onto her bed, punching her fists into the pillow.

Finally she calmed down enough to go back to her desk. She picked up her pen and wrote after "to be continued":

Guess what? A minute ago Germs, Inc. left our house. She came here with a petition to get rid of the

*new people. I wanted to kick her in the guts!!! I'm so
mad I don't know what to do.*

Winnie folded the letter and put it in the middle
of the world atlas. She didn't know how to finish it.

She undressed and climbed into bed. She didn't
bother brushing her teeth or washing her face. She
put out the light and tried to sleep. Maybe things
would seem better in the morning.

Winnie sat at the kitchen table and pretended to
eat her breakfast. She used her "moving around"
method to make her mother think she was eating. Actually she had taken only two mouthfuls of scrambled
eggs. The rest she had moved around and around on
her plate.

"Are you finished moving those eggs around
Winnie?" Mom asked.

Winnie looked up. So her special, secret trick
was not going to work this morning. It figured! "You
really aren't supposed to eat much when it's hot, you
know, Mom. I read that someplace."

Mrs. Barringer smiled. "You certainly do use
any and every excuse for not eating." She was interrupted by a loud bark. Mrs. Barringer looked out the
kitchen window. "That's funny. There's nothing
there! I was sure I heard a dog barking. I don't want
any dogs around my rose bushes."

Winnie paid no attention to what her mother was saying. She continued to move the eggs around, making little yellow designs on her plate. The barking began again.

"Winnie, don't you hear that?" her mother asked.

"Sure Mom."

"Check out front Winnie, will you?"

"Okay . . . okay." Winnie went to the front door and looked out. She didn't see a thing, so she headed for the garage and her bike. She might as well ride around. She was still confused about last night. But at least she had reached one decision. She would never mention that awful petition to the Garbers. Maybe no one would sign it and they would never have to know. Suddenly Winnie heard a loud "WOOF." It startled her and she spun around looking for the dog. Then she heard somebody laughing. It sounded like it was coming from inside the garage. Winnie ran over to the side window and peeked into the dark garage. She couldn't really see anything. So she opened the garage door, very slowly and very carefully. She wasn't quite sure what she might find inside. "Oh no!" she hollered when the door was opened. "How did you get in here?"

A loud "WOOF . . . WOOF" was the only reply. The red wagon that she forgot to take home yesterday was in the middle of the garage. Sitting in the middle of the red wagon was a dog. It looked like a huge stuffed Panda bear with shaggy white fur (except for one black eye and one black ear). "Okay, I know somebody's in here. Come on out! Right now!" she commanded.

Somebody giggled. Then somebody else giggled. And finally Tina, Herbie and Glenn jumped out from behind Mr. Barringer's gardening supplies, where they were hiding.

"Hi Winnie," they yelled.

"How do you like our furry friend?" laughed Glenn.

Herbie jumped up and down. "I told you Winnie. I told you we were going to get him last night. Isn't he something?" Herbie seemed excited about the dog. Yesterday he'd acted so *blah*.

"Is he ever!" Winnie agreed. "He's really neat! But he's so big!"

"You think this is BIG?" Glenn asked. "He's only a puppy now. 'Course he already weighs forty pounds. How about that!"

"Wow . . . some puppy!" Winnie said. "What kind of dog is he anyway?"

"This is a Sheep Dog," Tina announced. "A genuine English Sheep Dog puppy."

"Ha! A Sheep Dog!" Winnie laughed. "That's funny. That's really very funny. I never saw one before. But that's what my Mom says I look like when I don't brush my hair. Look!" And Winnie shook out her long hair, letting it fall over her face, covering her eyes. She danced around the wagon hollering, "WOOF! Woof . . . Woof . . . Woof . . . !" She collapsed on the floor laughing.

At first the dog seemed confused. He stood up in the wagon and began rocking back and forth. Then he bellowed . . . long and low. "Arooo . . . Arooo . . . WOOF"—and jumped out of the wagon onto Winnie. "Oh help!" Winnie called out. "Get this monster off me!" But the dog was busily licking Winnie's nose and ears. Glenn and Herbie tried to pull him off. Tina joined her brothers and they all tugged at once. After much grunting, groaning and barking they managed to separate the dog from his new friend.

Tina brushed off Winnie's clothes which were covered with shaggy white hairs. "Never again!" Winnie promised. "I'm never playing doggie again! Let's get out of here now before my mom catches us. She's not big on dogs running loose around here. They're not good for her rose bushes, if you know what I mean."

"Okay," Glenn said. "Let's take him for a walk."

"Why do you call him HIM?" Winnie asked, as

they started walking. "Doesn't the dog have a name?"

Glenn didn't answer. Neither did Herbie or Tina. But they all giggled. Winnie put her hands on her hips and said, "Well, if you're not going to tell me I'm not going for a walk with you!"

"Oh, we'll tell you, Winnie," Glenn assured her. "It's just a kind of different name. That's all."

"Okay, so it's different. I don't mind," Winnie said. "What is it?"

"We wanted to call him SMREG," Tina said.

"SMREG?" Winnie asked, "SMREG?" What kind of name is that for a dog? That's really crazy! What'd you want to call him that for?"

The Garbers laughed again, and this time Winnie was annoyed at being left out of the joke.

Glenn stopped laughing long enough to tell her. "SMREG is GERMS spelled backwards!"

"GERMS SPELLED BACKWARDS!" Winnie repeated loud enough for the whole block to hear. "Oh, that's too much! That's really great! Too bad it makes such an awful name for a dog! Here Smreggie," Winnie called, trying it out. "Good doggie. Here, nice Smreg." She laughed as hard as the others. Finally she remembered that she still didn't know his name. She stopped laughing and asked, "So what *is* his name?"

Glenn cleared his throat and took a deep bow.

"Introducing," he said . . . "Introducing Woozie Garber."

Winnie stared down at the shaggy, white dog who sat scratching himself at her feet. She shook her head and mumbled, "Woozie . . . Woozie . . . Woozie. What a name! It's almost as bad as Smreg!" The dog looked up and barked at her. "Okay . . . okay," Winnie told him soothingly, while patting his back. "Woozie is a lovely name. Lovely! And you're a lovely doggie! Where'd you ever get a name like Woozie anyway?" she asked Glenn.

Tina looked at the ground and shuffled her feet. Herbie and Glenn smiled. "Go ahead Tina," Herbie insisted. "Go ahead and tell Winnie."

"Okay, okay," Tina said softly, still looking down. "See, when I was real little I had this stuffed dog that I used to take to sleep with me and I called him Woozie and . . ."

"You've still got that old thing Tina," Herbie accused, interrupting his sister. "I saw you with it the other night."

Tina put her hands on her hips and looked straight at Herbie. "Oh sure I've still got him. But I don't *use* him anymore. He's in this box in my closet and sometimes I like to take the box down and JUST LOOK AT HIM. That's all!"

Herbie and Glenn laughed some more. Tina

chewed her bottom lip. Winnie felt sorry for her. "That's not so funny," she told the boys. "When I was little I had an old blanket I dragged around. I dragged it around for years, till it fell apart. And I called it Blangley. Anyway, I changed my mind. I think Woozie is a great name for him. He looks like a Woozie." Tina smiled a private thank you to Winnie. Woozie jumped up and barked his approval. Then he suddenly took off like a rocket and ran down the block.

"You naughty old doggie! You come back here!" Tina hollered after him. But Woozie had already run up the Landon's front walk. She poked her brother. "Go get him Glenn."

Glenn looked at Herbie. "Herbie can run faster than me. Go get him Herbie."

But Herbie looked at Tina. "Let Tina get him. She's the youngest and she's always complaining about how she NEVER gets to do anything. Right, Tina?"

Tina looked at Winnie pleadingly. "Well, I see I'm elected dog catcher," Winnie said. "I'm not scared of Germs, Incorporated!" She popped a fresh piece of gum into her mouth, pulled her sailor hat down over her ears, and ran to the Landon's house.

She paused before continuing up the front walk, wondering why Woozie decided to visit the worst possible house on the block. She looked around. No Woozie. She thought hard about where he might be, then snapped her fingers, remembering the Collie that lived behind the Landon's. At that moment Clarice opened the door and stepped out onto the front porch. She was sucking an ice cube and it was dripping onto her pink and white dress. Winnie nodded at her and cracked her gum.

"Hi Winnie. Want to play?" Clarice asked timidly.

Winnie shook her head from side to side and cracked her gum louder. "That's disgusting Winifred!" Clarice said between slurps.

"So's sucking on an ice cube!" Winnie answered.

"Well, if you don't want to play, what are you doing here?" Clarice asked.

"Oh, just looking for a dog is all," Winnie said.

"What dog?" Clarice wanted to know.

And that was when Woozie chose to show himself. He appeared around the corner of the house, ran over to Winnie, looked up at Clarice and began to bark furiously.

"Mommy!" Clarice screamed. "Mommy! There's a big dog after me! Help, Mommy . . . HELP!"

Winnie grabbed Woozie by the collar and tried

to persuade him to leave quietly with her. But Woozie kept barking and Clarice kept screaming until Mrs. Landon came to the door. Clarice hid behind her mother's back.

"Winifred Barringer, what are you doing on our front walk with that dog?" Mrs. Landon asked.

Oh boy, Winnie thought. Here we go! She stood up straight and faced Mrs. Landon. "He ran away and I'm just trying to catch him, is all."

"Ran away from whom, Winifred? Exactly whose dog is he?" Mrs. Landon demanded.

"He's the Garbers' dog," Winnie said, biting her lip.

"The Garbers' dog! I see. Please get him out of here, Winifred. I could report the Garbers for letting their dog run loose. I could very well do that."

"Oh, please don't, Mrs. Landon. They just got him and it was *my* fault . . . really." She *would* do something like that, Winnie thought. She just would!

"Very·well, Winifred. I see no reason to be nasty." Out came the smile. "But I never want this to happen again. Is that clearly understood?"

"Yes, Ma'am. Clearly."

Woozie meekly followed Winnie down the Landon's walk as if he had understood all of what Germs had said. She never even raised her voice, Winnie thought. She can be rotten without even trying!

chapter five

The next morning Winnie got up at eight. She read over the letter she'd started to Iggie. It sounded stupid. She ripped it up and started again:

Dear Iggie,

How are you? I'm fine. You'll never believe this but the Garbers (our new neighbors) who moved into your house got a sheep dog. Anyway, his name is Woozie and today he ran off and where did he run to of all places? You guessed it—the Landon's!!! Well, Mrs. Germs was really mad. Actually, she was really mad because she doesn't like the Garbers. Well, it isn't exactly that she doesn't like them because she *doesn't even* know *them. It's just that she doesn't want them around because they're Negro. (They say black.)*

"Winnie! Breakfast," her mother called.

Winnie folded the letter and put it under her school papers in her middle desk drawer.

Later that morning Winnie, Herbie, Glenn and Tina sat on the curb, in front of the sewer grating that was next to Iggie's driveway. Winnie reached over and picked up some pebbles from the hole at the foot of the driveway. Iggie's folks had been planning to fix up that hole in the fall. Winnie threw the little pebbles into the sewer, one by one. They made a clinking sound.

The Garbers looked glum. Nobody had anything to say. Winnie wished she had stayed home and slept all morning. "What's eating you guys?" she finally asked.

"Nothing much," Glenn answered.

"Well, it must be *something*," Winnie said.

Herbie jumped up, imitating his brother. "Oh nothing much . . . nothing much is wrong . . . like fun it's nothing much!" His voice got very gruff and his fingers automatically went up to his mouth. He started gnawing away at his nails and it was hard to understand what he was saying. "Just a little old piece of paper with a lot of names on it telling the Garber family to get lost. That's about all! *Nothing much!*"

The petition! They knew about Mrs. Landon's petition. Winnie didn't know what to say. "I'm uh . . . I mean I . . . uh . . ." she stammered.

Herbie slapped his leg. "Didn't I tell you? Didn't I tell you she wouldn't be surprised. I told you she'd know about it!" he said to his brother.

Glenn held up his hand. "Don't try to explain, Winnie. Please! We don't want to hear a lot of excuses."

Explain! That was funny. How could she explain a Mrs. Landon? How could she explain why her own mother didn't want them on her block? How could she explain anything? She didn't even understand it herself. "How did you find out?" she asked.

Glenn reported, "Germs, Incorporated paid us a little visit last night. My mother invited her in."

"But didn't you tell her about Mrs. Landon? About how she told Clarice not to play with any . . ." Winnie stopped.

"Well, go ahead. Go ahead and say it!" Herbie shouted. "Any *colored* kids!" He spit the words out.

"Leave her alone Herbie. It's not her fault."

Winnie spoke to Glenn, ignoring Herbie. "But why didn't you tell your mother? You should have warned her."

"We should have, but we didn't. She's so

jumpy lately that we decided not to give her the news."

"So your mother just let her in. Just like that?"

"Yeah," Herbie said, joining the conversation again. "Mom thought Mrs. Landon was being polite and calling on her new neighbor."

"You should have seen old Germs," Glenn said. "She was taking it all in. Couldn't look around fast enough. Then she announced that she wants to talk privately to my folks. That means me and Herbie are supposed to take off."

"What about Tina?" Winnie asked.

"I was in the bathtub," Tina sighed. "I always miss everything!"

Glenn continued. "So me and Herbie slammed the back door, pretending to go out into the yard. But we really stayed in the kitchen and we heard the whole thing."

"What'd she say?" Winnie asked.

"Oh, how she's sure we're *lovely* people and that it's nothing personal, but we'd be happier somewhere else. For the children's sake and all that jazz."

"Then what?" Winnie asked Herbie.

"Then my father says he's heard enough. And would she please leave. All very nice and quiet. . . . Man! You'd have thought they were talking about the weather or something. Then Mrs. Landon says,

'Oh, I almost forgot . . . we've gotten a petition to-gether so that you can see how we really feel about the situation.' And she hands it over to my father."

"Did you see the petition?" Winnie asked. She'd absolutely die if her parents signed it.

"Yeah," Herbie said. "I snitched it out of my father's desk this morning."

"How many signed it?" Winnie was petrified.

"Only nine," Glenn said.

"ONLY?" Herbie raised his voice.

"Nine out of thirty two . . . that's not a lot," Glenn argued.

"Man! It's enough!"

"Do you remember all the names?" Winnie whispered. She'd faint if her family's name was on it.

Herbie picked up a handful of pebbles and threw them into the sewer. "If you want to know if your parents signed it . . . they didn't!"

"I never even thought of that, Herbie Garber!" Winnie hollered. She hoped the relief she felt didn't show. "What are you going to do about it?" she asked.

"I know what I'd like to do," Herbie said. "For a start I'd break up some windows on the Germ House. Then maybe I'd dump some paint on that nice green grass. And I'd train Woozie to make on all her bushes!"

"And what would that prove, big shot?" Glenn asked.

"Maybe nothing. But man! It would sure make me feel good!"

"I meant what are your folks going to do about it?" Winnie asked.

Herbie scratched his head. "Who knows? They don't let us in on anything. We're not supposed to know about the petition. It's called 'protect the children from everything bad in the world.' Just close your eyes and it'll all go away."

"I know the feeling," Winnie admitted. "Do your parents whisper a lot at night . . . when you're all supposed to be asleep?"

"Yeah," Glenn said.

"Why can't they ever be honest?" Winnie muttered.

"Who knows!" Herbie said. "Who can figure out parents."

Winnie stood up and brushed off her shorts. "Well, we can't just sit here all day. What do you guys want to do?"

"How 'bout the park?" Tina asked.

"Too crowded on Saturdays," Winnie answered.

"We could take Woozie out for a walk," Herbie suggested.

"Say! I know . . . Iggie's tree house," Winnie said. "Have you guys discovered it yet?"

"What tree house? Where is it?" Tina asked.

"In your yard, silly. Come on . . . follow me." Winnie and Tina ran into the backyard. Glenn and Herbie followed slowly. The tree house was practically invisible among all the leaves of Iggie's tall trees. "Iggie's father built it for us last summer. All by himself, except for me and Iggie. We helped him," Winnie said, pointing it out.

"Do you have binoculars?"

"What's binoculars?" Tina asked.

"Binoculars are what you look through to see things far away. It makes everything look close. Right, Glenn?" Herbie asked, turning to his brother.

"Right, Herbie. But I don't think we have any," Glenn said.

"Okay. Wait here and I'll go get mine," Winnie told them, running off toward her house. She was in and out in about two and a half minutes. Just long enough to dash up the stairs, take her binoculars lovingly from the dresser drawer, where she kept them hidden under her pajamas, and fly back down the stairs and out the kitchen door with them. When she got back she sniffed in the delicious smell of Iggie's mom's flowers. They were all in bloom. She hoped Mrs. Garber would take good care of them.

"Hello down there," Glenn sang out.

Winnie looked up. Herbie and Glenn were already in Iggie's tree house. Winnie felt kind of funny about it. It used to be her's and Iggie's special place. But she guessed Iggie wouldn't mind. Probably her father was busy building her a new tree house in Tokyo. If they had trees there!

"Where's Tina?" Winnie asked the boys, as she climbed up the rope ladder to the wooden planks that made up the floor of the tree house.

"She went inside for a minute, with our Dad," Herbie said. "He's off on Saturdays. Isn't your father?"

"No. Saturday's a big day for hardware stores." Winnie said. She never thought much about Mr. Garber. She had only seen him once. That day she was spying on them when they moved in.

"Well, here's my binoculars," Winnie announced. "Want to see?"

Herbie took them and held them up to his eyes. He moved them around and handed them back disgustedly. "Some fun. All I see are tree tops and leaves."

"Oh Herbie," Winnie laughed. "You're not looking in the right places. Here Glenn, have a turn."

Glenn put the binoculars to his eyes. He moved them around and adjusted the focus. "Boy! These are really powerful!"

"I know it." Winnie agreed. "Iggie gave them to me for my birthday last year. They used to belong to her uncle who's in the Marines. Here, give them to me a minute and I'll show you something." Glenn handed them to her. Winnie stood up and waved her free hand around, while holding the binoculars in the other. "Points of interest up and down Grove Street are . . ." she announced in a deep and dramatic voice.

"Number one: The man who lives behind here and three doors down. I forget his name, but he mows his lawn in a red bathing suit every week. On Thursdays, I think. And he's real fat and his belly jumps all around when he pushes the mower. He's not out today . . . too bad!

"Number two: Pay attention please, Herbie Garber." Herbie took his fingers out of his mouth and looked at Winnie, who then continued her speech.

"Three doors down and on the right. Mrs. Axel's yard. Completely fenced in. Nobody knows what Mrs. Axel does all day in her fenced-in yard but me and Iggie. You want to know? Well, she sunbathes in there. Sunbathes and talks on the phone. She's got this outside phone connection and she gabs, gabs, gabs all day long. You know what she wears? A towel! That's it. Just a towel and the telephone. That's Mrs. Axel!"

Winnie turned and faced the other way. She

pointed with one hand as she peered through the binoculars. "Number three: Billy Mesler. One and a half
years old. We just discovered him this summer. He
climbs out of his playpen which is in the middle of
his yard. He crawls into the flower beds and eats. He
eats flowers, dirt and stones. Sometimes all three at
once. Mrs. Mesler comes outside screaming when she
discovers Billy is out of his playpen. She finds him
eating dirt and stuff and then she starts to cry. She
picks him up, washes out his mouth, puts him back
into his pen and pretty soon the whole thing starts
over again."

"You sure do know a lot about what goes on
around here!" Glenn said.

"Yes, I sure do!" Winnie agreed.

The back door slammed and Tina and Woozie
came out. "Hello down there," Winnie called to
them.

"Hi Winnie," Tina answered. "Come on down
here for a second. I want to show you something."

Winnie handed her binoculars to Glenn, in-
structing both boys to be very careful with them, but
to holler if they saw anything special. She climbed
down the rope ladder and ran over to Tina and
Woozie who were still standing by the back door.
She bent down to scratch Woozie behind the ears but
backed away. "Yick! What's the matter with him.
He smells funny and his fur's all sticky!"

"That's what I wanted to show you. It's this stuff called *No-Shed*. Daddy got a bottle of it for Woozie 'cause his fur is shedding all over the house already and we've only had him one day! So I rubbed it all over him. And now look—he's a mess! What do you think?"

"I think you're right. He's a mess. You better ask your father about him," Winnie suggested.

Tina yelled into the house. "Daddy, could you come out for a second?"

"What is it now Tina?" a deep voice called up from the basement.

"It's Woozie, Daddy. I think he needs you!" Tina hollered.

Winnie heard heavy steps coming up from the cellar. Then Mr. Garber appeared, looking both hot and tired.

"Daddy, this is Winnie, from down the street," Tina said, still staring at her dog.

"Hello Winnie," Mr. Garber said, glancing from Winnie's face to Woozie's sticky fur.

"Hi Mr. Garber," Winnie answered as Tina's dad bent down to inspect Woozie.

"Whatever happened to him?" Mr. Garber asked, looking up at Tina, from where he kneeled beside the dog.

"Oh Daddy!" Tina sniffled. "I wanted to take care of him so I rubbed the whole bottle of

61

No-Shed on his fur. To make him stop shedding Daddy. So Mom wouldn't be mad at him for messing up the house."

Mr. Garber sat down on the back stoop, threw his head back and laughed. He laughed deep and loud. Winnie and Tina looked at each other. If there was a joke they didn't know what it was. "What's so funny Daddy?" Tina finally asked.

"Tina, come over here," her father said in between laughs. She sat down on her father's lap. "Tina, you don't rub *No-Shed* on his fur. You put a teaspoon of it into his drinking water each day."

"Oh Daddy!" Tina wailed. "Did I hurt him? Will Woozie die?"

"I'm sure he'll recover Tina. He'll need a good bath and then he'll be fine. But next time you want to help, *please* ask first, okay?"

"Okay, Daddy." Tina hugged her father.

"Hey down there," Herbie called. "Something's up. Germs, Incorporated is carrying some kind of sign and heading our way. Have a look, Glenn."

"Yeah, here she comes—marching down the street. And Clarice is right behind her. Just skipping along. I can see them real good. Mrs. Germs is wearing a red hat with cherries on top of it."

"I can't read the sign—she's got it turned the wrong way," Herbie announced, without bothering to look through the binoculars. "Come on," he called, "let's go see!"

Both boys scurried down the rope ladder from the tree house and joined Winnie and Tina, who were already hiding behind one of the big evergreen bushes. Mrs. Landon was hammering the sign into the lawn with her shoe. The cherries were dangling from her red hat and Clarice stood by, sucking a lollypop. Mrs. Landon stood back to admire her work, brushed off her hands, put her shoe back on and continued marching down the street. Clarice followed like an obedient little lamb.

Winnie, Tina and the boys ran down to have a look. Mr. Garber came around to the front just as Herbie picked up a stone and hurled it at the sign. "I HATE HER!" he screamed. "I hate her, I hate her, I hate her! She doesn't even know us. She's never even talked to us! I wish I was back in Detroit where everybody's black!" Herbie ran sobbing toward the house.

Glenn read the sign in a hoarse and whispery voice, as if he needed to say it out loud to believe that it was real.

GO BACK WHERE YOU BELONG. WE DON'T WANT YOUR KIND AROUND HERE!!!!!

Mr. Garber grabbed the sign, yanked it out of

63

the ground and broke it in half over his knee. Winnie felt her cheeks burning. She was shaking all over. "We're not all like that," she heard a small voice say. "We're not . . . we're not . . . we're not." She realized the voice was her own and that she was crying. She turned and fled, tears streaming down her face.

chapter six

Winnie opened her eyes and looked around. For a second she was not quite sure where she was. Then she remembered runing home from the Garbers. She remembered the way she had burst through the back door of her house and how her mother had chased her up the stairs, two at a time. She knew that now she was sprawled out on her bed and that no one had taken the time to fold back the blue quilted spread. Her mother was bending over her and there was a cold, wet washcloth on her forehead. Winnie rolled her eyes from side to side.

"Thank heavens, Winnie!" Mrs. Barringer sighed. "Can you tell me what hurts?"

"Everything hurts," Winnie moaned.

The expression of relief left Mrs. Barringer's

face. She got up off the bed. "I'm going to call the doctor," she announced, "and I'll be right back."

Winnie reached out and caught her mother's arm. "Don't leave Mom. Please stay here," she whimpered.

"It will only take a minute, Winnie."

But Winnie sat up and shouted, "I don't want him Mom. I don't need any doctor. I'm not sick like that!" She put her head back down on the pillow and moaned again.

"Are you sure you're not sick Winnie?" Mrs. Barringer sat down on the bed beside her, feeling her forehead.

"No, I am not sick!" Winnie insisted.

"Well then, what happened? You came into the house screaming and crying. Something must have happened. Let's talk about it."

Winnie sat up again. "Do you know what she did Mom? Do you know?" she asked breathlessly. "She put a sign in their grass. A SIGN! Can you imagine! She's the most horrible person that ever lived! And I hate her!" Winnie flopped backwards and stared up at the ceiling.

"What are you talking about?" Mrs. Barringer asked, shaking her head. "I haven't any idea. You're not making sense." She handed Winnie a tissue. "Here, blow your nose and let's start over again."

Winnie sat up. She blew her nose hard, took a deep breath, and blurted out the whole dreadful story. When she had finished, her mother studied her face for a moment without speaking. Then Mrs. Barringer sighed and said, "What an awful thing to do." She put the washcloth back on Winnie's forehead, and brushed some loose strands of hair off her face. "But I certainly am relieved to find out there's nothing wrong with you. You had me worried Winnie!"

Winnie jumped back up. "Nothing wrong? How can you say that! Everything is wrong. EVERYTHING! Didn't you hear what I just said? I ran away when I read the sign. I ran away Mom. I didn't even say anything. I just ran. They'll probably hate me now. I could just die!"

Mrs. Barringer laughed softly. "Oh Winnie! You're being ridiculous. I think you're making too much out of the whole thing. Why should they hate you?"

Winnie looked straight into her mother's eyes. "Why should they hate me?" she asked. "That's easy. I'll tell you why. Because I'm white!"

"Winifred! You are not thinking. Mrs. Landon is one person. You are another! No one is going to hate you for running away!" Mrs. Barringer insisted.

"But Mom . . . maybe they'll think we're all like Mrs. Landon. She hates the Garbers and she doesn't even know them! So maybe the Garbers will think we're all the same! We've got to prove it to them Mom."

"Prove what, Winnie?" Mrs. Barringer asked.

"Prove that we're not all like Mrs. Landon!" Winnie said, throwing her hands up into the air.

"Winnie!" Mom sighed, annoyed. "You're carrying this thing too far. You're devoting all your time and energy to the Garber cause. You've got to learn to think things through. You're always jumping into new situations with both feet, before you know what you're jumping into!"

"But Mom . . ." Winnie began.

"Just a minute. Just one minute, please. I'm not through yet," Mrs. Barringer said. "Do I have to remind you that last year you started the Freedom for Turtles Club? And as President you went around ringing all the doorbells on Grove Street, telling people how wrong it was to keep little turtles cooped up inside a house. Well, do you remember that Winnie?"

Winnie felt her cheeks redden. "Oh Mom! I was only ten then. And anyway, it's true about turtles. They should be free to walk around outside."

"But my point is that it's still the same thing. You're jumping into something that you know nothing about." Mrs. Barringer shook a finger at her daughter.

68

"The same thing! How can you say that?" Winnie asked furiously. "Turtles are turtles! But these are people Mom. PEOPLE! Sometimes I think you're just like Mrs. Landon," Winnie mumbled disgustedly.

"That is completely unfair of you Winnie!" her mother answered angrily. "Why, I would never dream of behaving the way Mrs. Landon has."

"Well then, why don't you do something?" Winnie asked, raising her voice.

"Do what? What is it you want me to do?"

Winnie pleaded. "Anything Mom. Anything to prove we're different. Anything to show we're interested."

"Listen to me Winifred," Mrs. Barringer argued. "These people must have known they'd have problems to face when they moved here."

"Well, why don't you help them solve their problems?" Winnie screamed. "I don't see how you and Daddy can just sit there day after day doing nothing. Are you against the Garbers?"

Mrs. Barringer did not reply.

"Well, are you?" Winnie asked again.

"No, Winnie," her mother answered in a calm voice. "We are definitely not against the Garbers."

"Then why don't you do something?" Winnie repeated.

"Because it really isn't any of our business, Winnie. Your father and I don't believe in getting mixed up in other people's lives. These things will work themselves out. Daddy and I are not crusaders."

"What do you mean crusaders?" Winnie asked, baffled.

"That's what you are Winnie. You're a crusader. Always finding a new cause and then jumping right in to fight for it. You're like Mrs. Landon in a way." Winnie glared. How dare her mother say that! Mrs. Barringer got off the bed. "I'm going to fix some lunch now. Oh, I almost forgot to tell you that Aunt Myrna called. She's invited you to her Swim Club this afternoon."

"I'm not going!" Winnie announced, staring up at the ceiling.

"That's up to you. But I do think it would be good for you to get away from here for one afternoon," Mrs. Barringer said as she left the room.

Winnie rolled over on her side and faced the wall. Aunt Myrna and her pool seemed very unimportant at the moment. Even if Winnie did know a lot of the people who belonged to it. Even if she usually jumped at the chance to go. Her aunt had taken her and Iggie practically once a week all summer. It was fun. Aunt Myrna wasn't bad either, considering that she didn't know much about kids. Aunt Myrna never bothered her when she was swimming. She didn't care much about what she and Iggie did at the pool as long as they didn't drown. And she never told them they were blue and had to come out of the water. Aunt Myrna was too busy playing cards with her friends to notice anything like that.

Winnie wondered if her aunt knew that Winifred Bates Barringer, her very own niece, was a CRUSADER! She wondered too if Aunt Myrna knew about the problems on Grove Street. Winnie's guess was that Aunt Myrna knew all about everything. After all, she was her mother's sister.

Winnie rolled over onto her stomach. How could her mother say she was like Mrs. Landon? That was crazy! She hated Mrs. Landon! Suddenly, the most brilliant idea of the week popped into her head. If she *was* like Mrs. Landon, then maybe she should petition too. Winnie smiled and jumped up from the bed. She opened her bottom dresser drawer and took out her favorite bathing suit. The orange one with the brass buttons up the side. She undressed, slipped into the suit, and pulled her sweat shirt on over her head. She sat down at her desk. First she crumpled up her letter to Iggie and threw it away. She took out a fresh sheet of yellow paper. At the rate she was going she'd have all envelopes and no paper pretty soon.

Dear Iggie,
How are you? I'm fine but I'm positively mixed up about everything!!! My mother just called me an-

*other Mrs. Landon. Can you imagine???? Sometimes
I can't stand my mother!! I've got loads to tell you
but right now I've got to run.*

She didn't bother hiding this letter inside a book
or under papers. She left it right on top of her desk.
Then she carefully tore a clean piece of white paper
from her notebook, and divided it into sections. She
nibbled on her pencil as she tried to decide how to
phrase her petition. Should she write "Negro," like
her teacher said? "Black," like the Garbers said? Or
"colored," like her parents said? She decided that
most of the people at Aunt Myrna's swim club acted
more like her parents than her teacher. And they certainly weren't like the Garbers! They were all white.
She printed across the top in capital letters:

FEELINGS ABOUT COLORED PEOPLE

Please check one:

YOUR NAME	LIKE	DON'T LIKE	DON'T CARE	DON'T KNOW

Winnie carefully folded her petition and tucked it into her red shoulder-strap pocketbook, along with a sharp pencil, her bathing hat and her nose clips. She skipped down the stairs humming and announced to her mother that she was ready to go to the pool.

"Well," Mom said with a smile. "You certainly changed your mind fast."

Winnie had no intention of sharing her plans with her mother. *She* wouldn't understand anyway.

"Call your aunt and tell her you'll be ready in a few minutes. First you've got to have some lunch."

"I'll call and tell her I'm ready now. I'm not hungry," Winnie said as she picked up the phone.

She sat on the front steps waiting for her aunt's red sports car. As it rounded the corner of Grove Street Winnie yelled, "Bye," to her mother and ran down to the curb. Aunt Myrna had the top down on the car. She wore big, red-framed sun glasses.

"Hop in Winnie and let's go," Aunt Myrna called. "Don't want to miss my bridge game."

Winnie and her aunt did not exchange one word on the fifteen-minute drive to the Swim Club. Winnie was busy thinking about her petition. As Aunt Myrna steered the car into a small parking space in the almost full lot she turned to her niece. "Are you okay Winnie? I've never seen you so quiet."

"Oh sure," Winnie answered, surprised that her

aunt had even noticed. "I'm just thinking, that's all."

"Your mother told me about your new friends," Aunt Myrna added.

"That's nice." Winnie was not about to give out valuable information that might get back to her mother.

They got out of the little car and walked toward the gate where Aunt Myrna had to show her membership card, even though she came to the pool every day and everyone knew her. Aunt Myrna signed the register and paid for one guest.

"Didn't you bring anything to change into Winnie?" her aunt asked.

"Nope. I'll dry off in the sun before we go home."

"Okay. Now remember, no drownings while I'm in charge! Here," Aunt Myrna said, pressing a dollar bill into Winnie's hand. "Go have a hot dog."

chapter seven

Winnie clenched Aunt Myrna's dollar bill in her sweaty hand. She kicked open the door of the screened-in refreshment stand and stepped inside, out of the hot sun. Here it was dark and cool. It took a minute for her eyes to adjust to the change before she was able to look around for a familiar face. There was none. She went up to the counter and waited for her turn. Two little kids were ahead of her. They were trying to decide between an ice-cream sandwich to share or a small candy bar for each of them. They counted their money again and again. Winnie began to tap her foot at them. She was starved. Her stomach was rumbling. The little kids looked up at her and finally asked for one bag of potato chips and a small raspberry sherbet. Winnie ordered a hot dog, french fries and a coke. She carried her lunch to a table in the corner. She had missed the usual Saturday lunch crowd and was glad of that. She hated to wait in line and get shoved around.

Winnie carefully decorated her french fries with just the right amount of ketchup and bit into the hot dog. It tasted marvelous. She patted her red pocketbook several times and then opened the clasp to make sure her petition was still here. It was.

"Well, look who's here," a familiar voice boomed. Winnie looked up just as Big Red pulled over a chair and sat down. "I'll join you," he announced, banging his coke down on her table.

"Are you asking me or telling me?" Winnie grinned.

"Um . . . don't mind if I do!" Big Red said, paying no attention to her. He helped himself to some of Winnie's french fries. After tasting one he reached for the ketchup. He smothered the rest of the potatoes in it and continued nibbling.

"Those WERE my french fries, you know," Winnie said. "And they WERE fixed the way I like them!"

"Oh, sorry Winnie. Didn't mean to spoil your lunch," Big Red said, munching.

Winnie sulked and concentrated on her hot dog.

When Big Red had finished stuffing himself with Winnie's potatoes he wiped his mouth with the back of his hand. "Why'd you feed me that goofy story about those colored kids? Why'd you tell me they were from Africa when you knew all the time they were just ordinary?" he asked Winnie. "And from Detroit!" he added disgustedly.

"Because I know how you are. That's why," Winnie said quietly, not looking up.

"What do you mean, how I am?" Big Red wanted to know.

This time Winnie looked directly into Big Red's blue eyes. "How you are about new kids. You never let new kids play right away. You make them suffer until you think they deserve the great privilege of playing ball with you."

"So you lied on purpose!" Big Red accused.

"It was just a joke, Big Red. Forget it!" Winnie said, sipping her soda.

"I hear you're real friendly with them," Big Red mumbled.

"So?"

Big Red shrugged and said, "So nothing! I just wondered. They seemed okay to me. I mean, what do I care what color they are, right?"

Winnie slammed her hand down on the table. "Right! What'd your folks say?" she asked.

"Nothing much. My mother said next thing you

know some nice girl from town will probably marry one."

"Oh . . . that's just great!" Winnie said, sarcastically.

"Yeah!" Big Red agreed. "But me, I'm not like that."

I'll bet, Winnie thought to herself, as Big Red got up and left the table. Winnie finished up her coke, threw the paper plates into the garbage can and walked out into the sunshine.

She parked herself on a chair at the side of the pool and pulled off her sweat shirt. She hung her nose clips around her neck, shaded her eyes from the sun and looked around. The swimming instructor, Mr. Berger, was on the far side of the rectangular pool. Winnie smiled and waved, but he didn't notice her. Mr. Berger taught physical education at the high school. Two years ago Aunt Myrna had given Winnie a present of a whole series of swimming lessons from him. He didn't approve of her nose clips, but she liked them because she never got water up her nose that way. Mr. Berger was walking in Winnie's direction. She stood up and held her pocketbook tightly.

"Hi Mr. Berger," she called out, waving.

"Well, Winnie! Glad to see you're doing all right without Iggie. Still got those old nose clips?

Time to get rid of them." He smiled good naturedly at her.

"Do you have a minute, Mr. Berger?" Winnie asked timidly.

Mr. Berger checked his watch. "Sure I do Winnie. My next lesson's not for another ten minutes." He sat down on a chair beside her.

"We've got some new neighbors Mr. Berger. In Iggie's house. They're uh . . . they're uh . . . Negro," Winnie said quietly.

Mr. Berger kept smiling at her. "Oh . . ."

"Yes . . . we're very good friends," Winnie said excitedly. Then she paused and added, "At least we were until this morning. Mr. Berger, I've got this petition and uh . . . I'd like you to sign it for me. Would you?"

Mr. Berger looked at Winnie for what seemed to be a very long time. Then he said, "Well, I can't answer that until I see it. Where is your petition?"

Winnie whipped it out and presented it to him. "Here it is and here's a pencil," she said, fumbling in the bottom of her pocketbook for the one she had sharpened so carefully.

Mr. Berger read her paper thoughtfully. "This is more of a questionnaire than a petition, Winnie. But I'll fill it out for you. He reached for her pencil and Winnie held her breath, wondering if he would check Like . . . Don't Like . . . Don't Care . . . or Don't Know.

Mr. Berger handed the questionnaire back to her. She was almost afraid to look. "Go ahead and read it Winnie," he said.

Winnie turned away from the sun and studied the paper. Mr. Berger had signed his name in the proper space: Frank G. Berger. To the question "Feelings about Colored People" Mr. Berger had written across one whole line . . . What color? Green or purple?

"Mr. Berger!" Winnie sighed, embarrassed. "You know what I mean!"

"Yes, I think I do Winnie. But I can't answer a question like that by checking a box. I have many feelings. And my feelings are different for each person."

"That's just it Mr. Berger!" Winnie raised her voice. Then she leaned over closer to him and explained softly, "You see, Mrs. Landon is being mean to the Garbers without knowing them, because of their color. And my folks, well, I'm disappointed in them too. And I'm all mixed up, Mr. Berger. And I just wish Iggie was here. And I wish somebody would help me understand!" Tears came to Winnie's eyes and she looked away.

"Winnie, Winnie," Mr. Berger said gently, putting an arm around her. "Sometimes life is like that. I'll tell you one thing though. I'm proud of you." And then with a grin he added, "Even if you do wear nose clips!"

"You think I'm right then?" Winnie asked, returning the smile.

Mr. Berger nodded. "I think anybody who cares about people is right Winnie."

They were interrupted by a shrill voice screaming, "Don't put your face near the water. Don't go in so deep. Come back here Clarice! You'll drown. No splashing! You'll ruin my hair. *Please* children!"

Winnie groaned, as she turned toward the voice. Mrs. Landon and Clarice. Yick! Winnie heard that they recently joined the pool. "I can't stand her," Winnie confessed to Mr. Berger. "And that itsy-bitsy precious-wecious little princess of hers!"

"I can understand how you feel about Mrs. Landon, Winnie. But try not to take it out on Clarice. It isn't easy to go through life with a mother like that. Why don't you talk to Clarice? Give her another point of view. The way Iggie did for you."

"I can't Mr. Berger. I just can't!" Winnie insisted.

"Well, think about it Winnie. I've got to give a lesson now. Keep your chin up!" Winnie nodded and watched Mr. Berger walk away.

She folded her questionnaire and tucked it into her pocketbook. Mr. Berger was right . . . you can't expect people to answer a question like that with a simple check mark. There had to be another way.

Winnie sat down on the edge of a lounge chair. She watched Mr. Berger jump off the diving board with a little boy. He used to do that with her too. She felt the sweat trickle down her chest inside her bathing suit. She decided as long as she was at the pool she might as well have a swim.

Winnie sat down next to the ladder at the deep end of the pool and dangled her feet in the cold water. She read the printed sign stating WOMEN AND GIRLS MUST WEAR BATHING HATS AT ALL TIMES—THE MANAGEMENT. She held hers in her lap, not wanting to put it on until the last possible second. The hat squeezed her head and she hated it.

Since she had passed the deep water test last summer she was allowed to use all sections of the pool. She even had a badge to pin on her bathing suit saying GUEST: DEEP WATER. Winnie was thinking about the things she and Mr. Berger had discussed when someone suddenly shoved her from behind and sent her splashing down into the cold water, totally unprepared. She came up choking and spurting water, her nose clips still hanging around her neck. The life guard stood up furiously blowing his whistle at her.

He pointed at her head, indicating that she was in the pool without a bathing cap. *Wonderful!* she thought! She might have drowned and all the life guard cared about was that her hair wasn't covered. She looked up into Big Red's laughing face.

"Oh, that was just great Winnie! I really surprised you, didn't I?" He laughed hysterically and slapped his thigh. "Oh boy, I really caught you off guard!"

Winnie muttered under her breath and considered how good it would feel to chop off his big red head with a sharp hatchet!

She climbed up the ladder, stepped out of the pool and sat down in the sun, hoping her hair dried before she had to go home. Mrs. Landon was still sitting on a chair right up close to the shallow end of the pool. She was wearing a bathing suit but had her sweater over her shoulders anyway.

Clarice was floating inside a tube. She twirled around and around but didn't get her face wet. At that moment Winnie felt sorry for her. Having a mother like Germs, Inc. was pretty bad. Mr. Berger was right. It really wasn't Clarice's fault that she was the way she was. Maybe when she got older she'd change. Maybe, but probably not, Winnie decided.

She took out her questionnaire again. She simply could not resist the temptation to approach Mrs. Landon. She walked over slowly and just stood there, waiting for Mrs. Landon to notice her.

"Hello, Winifred. Do you want to swim with Clarice?"

"No . . . I . . . uh . . . it's just my questionnaire, Mrs. Landon. I'd appreciate it if you would fill it out please," Winnie said, making her voice as gentle and sweet as she possibly could.

"Questionnaire! Now what are you up to young lady?" Winnie handed her the paper. Mrs. Landon read it and sucked in her breath. She kept her voice low, almost swallowing every word. "Winifred Barringer . . . I feel sorry for you! And for your parents!" Mrs. Landon shook the questionnaire in Winnie's face.

Winnie grabbed it and went to search for her aunt. She was afraid if she stayed she would cause a commotion. Then Aunt Myrna might be mad at her, and she was, after all, only a guest.

"Glad you're here Winnie," Aunt Myrna said, as Winnie approached her bridge table. "It's almost four o'clock, and I have to be going. Let's get our things together now."

Winnie opened the car door on the driver's side. She slid over into her own bucket seat, and fastened the safety belt. Aunt Myrna backed out of the parking lot and headed for Grove Street.

Winnie asked her aunt to drop her off at the Garbers, instead of at home. Aunt Myrna agreed. Winnie got out of the little red car, thanked her aunt for the afternoon, and skipped up to the Garbers' front door.

She pressed the bell and looked around. There was no green station wagon in the driveway. Winnie wondered if anybody was home. She pressed the bell again and listened for footsteps. She didn't know just what she was going to say to the Garbers, but she had to face them.

chapter eight

Glenn answered the door. "Hi Winnie," he said, munching a chocolate-chip cookie.

"Hi. Can I come in?"

"Sure. Why not?"

Winnie realized that she hadn't been inside the house since the Garbers moved to Grove Street. The thought gave her a sinking feeling, but she swallowed hard and stepped into the house. "Isn't anybody else at home?" she asked.

"Tina and my father took Woozie to the vet. He needed some shots." Glenn's voice was almost a whisper. Winnie had to lean close to hear every word. "And Herbie's upstairs sleeping." Glenn finished his cookie and brushed off his hands.

"Sleeping? At quarter to five in the afternoon? How come?"

"He puked after lunch. After uh . . . after Mrs. Landon . . . oh, you know." Glenn looked at his sneakers.

"Yeah," Winnie said, and then tried to brighten things up. "Say! I threw up on a bus once. Spaghetti! All over the place. The people on the bus weren't very happy about that at all." Winnie laughed nervously. She certainly hadn't planned to tell anyone that story.

Glenn didn't laugh. He just looked at her kind of funny. "I'm doing something in the kitchen . . . come on."

Winnie followed Glenn through the long hallway leading to the rear of the house. The kitchen looked out on the back yard. A folding table and three chairs were set up in one corner of the bright sunny room. Winnie sat down on a chair. The yellow countertops were cluttered with grocery bags. Somebody must have been shopping. Glenn reached into bag after bag, coming up with a variety of cans, jars and boxes, which he banged down on the counter. Winnie watched silently. She noticed that the Garbers used the same kind of peanut butter that her mother bought for her. The creamy kind. She hated the kind with lumps.

Glenn opened the cabinet over the counter and started putting in all the cans and jars. He didn't make rows like Mrs. Barringer did. He practically threw them in every which way. Winnie's mother lined everything up so you could read the labels.

"How come you're putting all that stuff away? Where's your mother?" Winnie asked.

"Upstairs," Glenn mumbled.

"What's going on around here anyway?"

Glenn faced her. "Okay, you might as well know, Winnie," he said disgustedly. "My mother's packing."

"Packing! For what?" Winnie asked.

"To leave here . . . to move . . . that's what!"

"But why?"

"Why!" Glenn raised his voice. "How can you ask why? You *know* why."

"You mean you're going because of . . . of . . . that sign and Mrs. Landon?" Winnie didn't want to believe it. How could the Garbers give up so easily?

"I don't know if we're really going or not. All I know is my mother's been screaming and carrying on all afternoon. She's had it! That's all I know."

"But what about you?" Winnie asked.

"Me!" Glenn laughed. "Do I matter? Does anybody ever care about what I think?" He turned back to the bundles.

"I do," Winnie said softly.

"A lot of good that'll do!" Glenn clunked two cans of tuna fish into the cabinet. "For all I know my mother's going to take us back to Detroit and leave my father here."

"Why would she do a thing like that?"

"Because my father's not going to *want* to move. I just know it. He's got the job he's been after . . . the one he's been working for."

"Your father's not mad?" Winnie asked.

"Mad!" Glenn slammed the cabinet door. "This is more than just getting mad. I don't think you understand."

Understand? What *did* he think anyway? Hadn't she been understanding right from the start. Wasn't she the one who wanted to be a good neighbor!

She heard somebody run down the stairs and tear through the hallway into the kitchen. It was Herbie. He looked awful. His eyes were red and swollen. He had a blue terry bathrobe wrapped around him. He was barefoot. Winnie hoped he wasn't going to throw up again. That was something she couldn't stand.

"Oh . . . it's *you!*" Herbie looked at her, then turned away.

"Come off it, Herbie," Glenn said. "There's no point in taking it out on Winnie."

"Good old Winnie!" Herbie slapped her on the back and made her cough. "Miss Do-Gooder Herself!"

Who did he think he was? Here she was trying to help . . . trying to do her best for them and this is where it got her. "Do you have to be so nasty all the time?" she asked Herbie. "What'd I ever do to you?"

Herbie dropped to his knees, pretending to pray. "Lord . . . oh Lord! Thank you Lord for sending the Garber family this Great Do-Gooder, Winifred. Now that she's discovered us, she's going to save us, Lord. All by herself! And after we're gone, Lord . . . then she'll be able to tell *everyone* how she's had black friends. Now isn't that wonderful! I ask you Lord . . . isn't that just too . . ."

Winnie jumped to her feet. "SHUT UP!" she yelled. "*Just shut up.*" She smacked Herbie across the face, as hard as she could. "YOU CREEP! she screamed. "*You rotten, lousy creep!*"

Herbie grabbed her by the arm. "Shut up yourself!" he hollered back.

Glenn stepped between Herbie and Winnie, forcing them apart. "Cut it out . . . both of you!"

"You know what I think, Herbie Garber," Winnie cried. "I think you're as bad as Mrs. Landon. I used to think you picked on me 'cause I'm a girl. But I just found out the truth. You hate everybody who's white! I feel sorry for you!" She stormed out of the kitchen before the tears came. They tasted hot and salty.

Glenn caught her at the front door. "Hey, take it easy Winnnie."

"Easy? Ha! Did I start it? Did I?"

"Look, all Herbie means is he doesn't think you'd be so interested in us if we weren't black. He doesn't want to be used by somebody who thinks it's groovy to have black friends."

"Doesn't want to be used! Well, I don't know what that's supposed to mean! I just don't seem to understand anything anymore!" She was crying hard now and she didn't care who knew it.

She ran home sobbing. Whatever made her think they were so special. They were just ordinary. That's all! Plain, old ordinary! And no matter how much she wanted to be friends . . . no matter how hard she tried . . . that Herbie Garber was hard to take! He was more than hard to take . . . he was IMPOSSIBLE.

Dear Iggie,

How are you? I have tried my absolute best to make friends with the Garbers (who bought your house). I have done everything I could for them. And do you think they appreciate anything???? They do not!!! Especially one impossible one named Herbie. I just smacked him. He's lucky I didn't kill him. I felt like it!!! What would you think of your best friend spending the rest of her life in jail?

Winnie took a bath before dinner. Nobody told her to, but if her folks saw how upset she was they'd want to know about it, and she wasn't going to go through that again. Not after this morning's scene with her mother.

She didn't feel like eating dinner. But her mother said, "No dinner . . . no dessert!" And Winnie had seen four cherry tarts sitting in the refrigerator. Her favorites! So she forced herself to nibble on the main course. She gagged on a mouthful of lima beans before she managed to wash them down with two glasses of water.

Just as her mother carried in the cherry tarts the doorbell rang. "I'll get it!" Winnie said, already out of her chair. "But don't start the tarts without me."

It was Mrs. Landon, *wearing* her glasses and looking very stern. "Good evening, Winifred. Are your mother and father at home?"

"Yes, but we're in the middle of dinner," Winnie said.

Mrs. Landon raised her voice. "Well then, I'll wait!"

Winnie could tell that Mrs. Landon was not about to leave so she went back into the dining room and announced the arrival of Germs, Incorporated.

"I guess our cherry tarts will have to wait," Mr. Barringer said, as they went to the front hall to greet Mrs. Landon. She wasn't there. She had already seated herself comfortably in the living room.

"Well, did you tell them, Winifred?" Mrs. Landon asked, turning on the smile.

"Tell us what?" Mrs. Barringer looked at Winnie.

"I don't know Mom," Winnie said.

"What you were doing at the pool!" Mrs. Landon said sharply.

Mr. and Mrs. Barringer looked at their daughter. Winnie said nothing.

"Well, if you don't tell them, I will! About your questionnaire," Mrs. Landon said.

"Oh that!" Winnie said weakly. "No, I didn't tell them about it. Not yet."

"Will somebody please tell *me* what is going on around here!" Mrs. Barringer demanded.

"I guess I'll have to be the one to tell you," Mrs. Landon began, before Winnie had a chance to say a word. "Your daughter—this child standing right here

—" she stood up and started to tap Winnie on the head with her handbag but Winnie ducked and moved away. "Your daughter brought a questionnaire to the pool today. And . . . and . . . she asked *me* to fill it out. Can you imagine!" Winnie had the feeling that Mrs. Landon was about to explode.

"What kind of questionnaire, Winnie?" Mr. Barringer asked.

"Wait a second and I'll get it Dad," Winnie said, dashing up the stairs.

She took the paper carefully out of her red pocketbook and smoothed it out. It had only one signature on it. Mr. Berger's. She carried it downstairs and presented it to her father, glancing sideways at Germs, Incorporated. She really wanted to stick out her tongue but her parents were watching.

Winnie's dad read the questionnaire, smiled and handed it to his wife. She read it and put it down on the coffee table, but did not smile.

"Well, she's not your child, Dorothy," Mr. Barringer said firmly, "and we don't need any help or advice in handling her. As for this questionnaire . . . I don't see any difference between it and your petition. Except of course you represent different opinions. But Winnie is as much entitled to an opinion as you are."

Winnie could hardly believe her ears. He was on

her side! Her father was on her side! He didn't like Mrs. Landon any more than she did!

"Well . . . well. . . ." Mrs. Landon fumed, her face turning purple. "I have news for you, Paul Barringer, that may make you change your mind. It just so happens that late this afternoon we had a real estate representative pay us a visit. He's going to do us a favor and buy our house. Of course we won't get as much as we should—because of THEM—but we feel fortunate in being able to get rid of it at any price. Now this gentleman is going to be calling on all of Grove Street very soon, offering to buy your homes quickly, while there is still time. And if you're smart you'll sell fast. Just as we did. Sell fast and get out of this neighborhood before it's too late! Before *they* take over!"

Mr. Barringer banged his fist on the top of the piano so hard that he shattered an ash tray and knocked over a vase. Water dripped onto the carpet but no one made a move to clean it up. Winnie thought her dad was going to lose control of himself. She had never seen him so mad. She didn't quite understand everything that Mrs. Landon was talking about but she got the general idea. The Landons were moving! She was glad to hear it.

Her father was shouting. "We'll have no Block-Busting on this street. No real estate agent's going to tell me I'd better sell my house. Not now and not ever! I WON'T HAVE IT! Nobody is going to scare me into selling because of the Garbers. Nobody!"

"Fine," Mrs. Landon shouted back. "I hope you and THEM will be very happy together."

"Why do you hate them so?" Winnie asked, joining in. "You don't even know the Garbers! So how can you hate them?"

"I don't have to know them!" Mrs. Landon screamed. "They're different . . . they're . . ."

"They are not," Winnie yelled, interrupting Mrs. Landon. "They even use the same kind of peanut butter. That's how different they are!"

There was absolute silence. The three grownups simply stared at her. Winnie wanted to grab Mrs. Landon and shake her. Then Mr. Barringer walked quickly to the front door and opened it. "Good night, Dorothy."

Mrs. Landon stomped out of the house. Winnie threw her arms around her father. "Oh Daddy! I'm so proud of you!"

"Look Winnie—I'm still not exactly sure about my feelings. I want you to understand that. But I'll tell you this. I'm going to organize a block meeting. Nobody else on this street is going to be pressured into selling his home. Not if I have anything to say about it. Now let's have those cherry tarts."

Winnie hadn't thought about her mother until now. When she looked over she saw her mother shaking. Her face was ashen. She frightened Winnie. "Mom?" Winnie said. "Mom? What's the matter?"

Mrs. Barringer covered her mouth with her hands and ran from the room.

Dear Iggie,

How are you? I hope you're fine because nobody around here is, especially my mother!!!

Yick! She wasn't in the mood. She'd finish it in the morning.

chapter nine

Winnie didn't sleep well that night. She was angry at her mother for behaving the way she did. Just like Herbie Garber! And furious that nobody got to eat any cherry tarts because of that awful Mrs. Landon.

The next morning when Winnie got up the house was perfectly still. No morning noises at all, even though the clock on her dresser said ten after nine. Then Winnie remembered it was Sunday. That was the trouble with summer. One day was just like another. It was hard to keep track of which was which. She dressed slowly and crept downstairs to the kitchen where she discovered her father, his nose buried in the Sunday papers. "Where's Mom?" Winnie asked.

"Sleeping," her father replied.

"Oh. She okay?"

"She will be. Just a little upset. Nothing to worry about."

"Oh."

"Your mother wants to move."

"But Daddy—we're not going to, are we? Last night you said . . ."

Her father interrupted her. "Sometimes people think more clearly in the morning."

It was her mother's fault. She'd gotten to him all right. Probably with one of those whispering campaigns. Everything her father stood up for last night was gone this morning. Vanished! *Poof!* Just like that!

Well, if they were going to move they were going to be in for a big surprise, because she wasn't going with them. She'd leave town . . . run away! She'd run to Iggie in Tokyo. At least Iggie's folks would understand. They'd take care of her. They'd never make her go back! And it wouldn't be hard. She'd hide on a ship. Hitch a ride to New York and then hide on a ship. She read about people who did that all the time. The only problem would be how to find Iggie once she got to Tokyo. Of course she had the address. All she'd have to do was find somebody who spoke English. Somebody to give her directions to Iggie's new house. Once she was there she'd never see her folks again. Maybe Matthew would join her. Yes, that was a good idea. She'd wait until Tuesday when Matthew came home from camp then they'd go together.

"Winnie! Why are you staring into space like that?" Mr. Barringer asked.

"What? Me? Oh, nothing!" Winnie poured pineapple juice from a can into a glass. "I think I'll make some plans if it's okay with you."

"Fine. Go ahead. No need to hang around here," her father answered.

She swallowed her juice in one gulp and walked out to the hall where she picked up the phone. Without thinking, Winnie started to dial Iggie's number. Of course it would have been changed! She called information and asked for GARBER . . . a new listing on Grove Street. She jotted down the number on the milk bill, which was lying face up on the telephone table.

She couldn't leave town without explaining it to them. Then Herbie would *really* have something to talk about! How she ran off when the going got rough. She'd show him. She'd show that Herbie Garber! She'd plan a day to remember.

The Garbers' phone rang twice before a gruff voice answered. "Hello . . . hello . . ."

Winnie hung up. She hadn't expected Herbie to answer. She waited a minute, then dialed a second time. "Hello . . . hello . . ." Herbie again.

Finally Winnie managed to say, "Hello Herbie. This is Winnie. May I please speak to Glenn?"

Silence on the other end. "Uh . . . Herbie . . ." Winnie continued. "Are you there?"

"Yeah. I'm here."

"Well, may I *please* speak to Glenn?"

"Just a second."

"Hello?" It was Glenn's voice.

"Hi. It's me . . . Winnie."

"I know."

"Oh. Well, it's a nice day and I was wondering what you were doing."

"Don't know."

"Oh."

"Why were you wondering?"

"Well, I thought we could do something together."

"Like what?"

"Maybe a picnic."

"Your house?"

"No, in the park."

"I thought you said the park's too crowded on weekends."

"Too crowded for ball . . . not to eat."

"Just you and me?" Glenn asked.

"No, everybody."

"Even Herbie?"

"Sure."

"Just a second." Winnie heard a lot of muffled voices in the background. Then Glenn said, "Okay, we'll go."

"Good!" Winnie was pleased. "Come over here as soon as you can. And Glenn, I'll bring everything we'll need for the picnic. Bye."

She hung up and raced back to the kitchen. Her father was gone. She slapped some peanut butter on eight slices of bread and carefully cut the sandwiches in half. She stepped back to admire her work. Yick! Whenever she cut with a knife it looked like she'd done the job with a dull scissors. The peanut butter sandwiches were no exception. She wrapped each sandwich in Saran, took an unopened box of chocolate-chip cookies from the pantry shelf, threw in a few napkins and put everything into a big brown paper bag. They could buy soda and ice cream at the stand in the park and if the Garbers had no money with them . . . well, Winnie would just treat them. She had plenty of allowance saved up.

She searched frantically for the picnic blanket but she couldn't find it upstairs or down. No use asking her father, who was in the den. Daddy never knew where anything was around the house. Instead, she pulled the blanket from her own bed, rolled it up, carried it downstairs, grabbed the brown bag of lunch and announced, "Daddy, I'm going to the park for a picnic. Just tell Mom I'll be home later this afternoon. Okay?"

"Fine. Bye," Mr. Barringer said without looking up. Winnie packed the red wagon with the blanket and lunch. She was outside and ready when the Garbers arrived. She couldn't look at Herbie. She'd never slapped anyone in the face in her whole life. She wondered if she should apologize, or what! But Herbie deserved that slap. He really did . . . so why apologize? She wasn't the one who started it. She'd do what her mother did after a fight with her father. Pretend it hadn't happened. Just act natural. "Hi," Winnie said.

Tina and Glenn answered, but Herbie was busy kicking a stone down the street.

"Let's go," Winnie said, pulling the wagon.

When they turned off Grove Street and onto Sherbrooke Road Winnie couldn't stand the suspense any longer. "Well, are you moving?" she asked Glenn.

"Nope."

"How come? What happened?"

"You've never seen our father when he's made up his mind about something!" Glenn said.

Herbie gave his stone a big kick, then turned

around to face the others. He pretended to be his father. He shook his finger at them and growled. "I've worked for years to get this job and I'm not giving it up now!"

"That's what he yelled at my mother," Tina whispered to Winnie.

Herbie continued his act. "Grow up honey! You've got to grow up and face life! Running away isn't the answer."

"That started my mother on a crying jag that lasted all night," Glenn added.

"But this morning she came down and gave us breakfast. She sniffled a lot but she didn't cry once," Tina reported.

"Man! Will I be glad when school starts. Anything to get out of that house!" Herbie kicked his stone.

"The Landons are moving," Winnie said, quietly.

"No kidding?" Glenn looked at her.

"Good riddance!" Herbie hollered. "Good riddance to the Germ family!"

"Mrs. Landon wants my folks to sell our house too."

They stopped walking. Winnie sat down on the edge of the wagon. Herbie, Tina and Glenn gathered around her.

"And?" Glenn asked.

"Well, I don't know yet," Winnie confessed.

Herbie bent over, picked up his stone and threw it. "Maybe we can start a nice little ghetto right on Grove Street. That's what it's all about, isn't it? Get out before *we* take over?"

"Look, I don't want to get into another fight," Winnie explained. "I just wanted to tell you that if my folks move away I'm not going with them."

"Where you going to live? In Iggie's tree house?" Herbie laughed.

"Very funny! I'm going to Tokyo. To live with Iggie's family."

"Oh, just like that! That's just great!" Herbie laughed at her again.

"Herbie, if you'd stop being so impossible for a minute . . ."

"Come on, Winnie!" Glenn said. "Going to Tokyo isn't exactly a practical idea."

"We'll see about that!" Winnie told them. "I already have my plans. I know how to do it. All you have to do is stow away on a ship. People do it all the time." Winnie jumped up off the wagon. She started to walk.

Sherbrooke Road was quiet today. No hammering, digging, or any of the usual building sounds. Winnie stopped in front of the first new house. She shaded her eyes from the sun and wondered who was going to live in it. "Want to go in and have a look around?" she asked.

"I don't think that's a very good idea," Glenn said. "Suppose we get caught?"

"It doesn't belong to anybody yet," Winnie said. "No one's working. And we're not going to do anything wrong anyway."

Glenn agreed. "Okay, but leave the wagon here, under the trees. Hey Herbie! We're going exploring. Come on!"

chapter ten

The four of them stepped along the wooden planks that had been stretched out like a walk so people could inspect the new houses without stepping on the muddy ground. At the end of the planks was a ladder, propped up against the brick porch. They climbed up one at a time.

The house was partitioned into rooms, but had no inside walls. They prowled through the first floor arguing about which room was which until they came to the kitchen. There was no doubt about that —a kitchen was a kitchen no matter what. Even without things like a refrigerator, stove and sink, they could still tell a kitchen. Next to it was a hole, leading to the cellar. They peered down into the darkness. There were no steps yet. Glenn held onto Tina's hand and motioned for them all to get away from the hole.

"Hey, let's play house," Tina said. "Winnie, you be the mother and Glenn's the father and Herbie's the baby and I'm Woozie. Woof - Woof."

"Okay doggie," Winnie said, chasing Tina up the stairs. "You know the rules—no dogs in the bedroom!"

Herbie and Glenn followed the girls to the second floor where they continued their exploring. There were two bathrooms back to back. They could tell because of the pipes. Winnie sat down on the floor in the corner pretending she was taking a bath. Herbie made a loud gargling sound.

They all laughed together and Winnie felt mighty pleased with herself. She took the credit for getting everyone friendly again. She really was the good neighbor she started out to be, wasn't she? Wait until she got to Tokyo and told Iggie's folks the whole story. Wouldn't they be proud of her!

"Let's go," Herbie called, after a few more minutes. "I'm hungry!"

"Me too," Winnie agreed.

They scrambled down the stairs and back outside, to where they had left the wagon with the blanket and the food.

When they got to the park Winnie led them to a grassy area under some tall trees. She spread out the blanket and opened the bag of sandwiches, handing one to each of her guests.

"This blanket itches me," Tina complained.

"Then sit on the grass," Glenn suggested.

"That itches me too."

"Then stand up," Herbie said, his mouth full of peanut butter.

"I don't like to eat standing up," Tina whined.

"Then don't eat!" Glenn hollered.

Tina plunked herself back on the blanket and picked up her sandwich. She finished it without another word.

"Peanut butter really makes me thirsty," Winnie said.

"Peanut butter makes *everybody* thirsty," Herbie agreed.

"And it sticks to the top of my mouth too," Tina said.

"Well, we have to walk down to the stand for drinks. I didn't bring them with me."

"Let's go," Glenn said, collecting the garbage into the brown bag.

Winnie led them down the path. She hummed a marching song. The day was really working out well. She was glad because she would be gone soon and she wanted Herbie and Glenn to remember her like this.

"Hey, there's a lake," Herbie called, when he reached the end of the wooded path.

"Yeah . . . and rowboats!" Glenn said.

"It's pretty isn't it?" Winnie asked, facing the round, blue lake. She looked around, admiring the flower beds. This was her favorite part of the park. Glenn, Herbie and Tina hadn't seen it the other day because the ball field was at the other end.

Herbie pointed. "Hey, look at those little kids fishing."

"I used to do that," Winnie said. "But I never caught anything. And they won't either." She laughed.

"Where are *they*?" Tina asked.

"Where are *what*?" Winnie answered.

"The black people."

Oh no! Tina was going to start *that* again! Winnie thought. "They aren't here today," Winnie told her. Why did Tina have to go and spoil things? Just when everything was going great!

"That's what you said the last time," Tina said.

"Tina, you dope!" Herbie shook his sister by the shoulders. "Don't you know by now? There just aren't any black people around here!"

"That's not true!" Winnie said. "There are some. And anyway, what's the difference?"

"The difference is . . ." Herbie let go of Tina

and faced Winnie. "How would you like it if you lived in a place where everybody was *black?*"

"I don't know."

"Come off it Winnie!" Herbie looked around and lowered his voice. "You know all right. You know!"

They were going to ruin her day. It wasn't fair! "You're the one making such a big deal out of it! Just remember that," Winnie said, walking toward the refreshment stand.

Herbie walked alongside her dragging his feet. "I'm not making a big deal. I'm just trying to be honest. That's what we wanted to be . . . remember? We all wanted people to be honest with us!"

"Four cokes," Winnie told the man behind the counter. She thought about what Herbie had said. It wasn't easy to be honest all the time. It really wasn't. Even if you wanted to.

The counter man put the four drinks in front of Winnie. "That'll be eighty-six cents," he said. "The six cents is tax."

Winnie fumbled around in her pocket.

"I'm paying," Glenn said, handing the man a dollar bill. "You brought the sandwiches," he told Winnie. "*I'm* buying the drinks."

Winnie looked up at him but didn't say a word. When Glenn finished his soda he wiped off his mouth and said, "You know what I feel like doing? I feel like going rowing!"

"I can't," Winnie said.

"Why not? Why can't you go?" Herbie asked.

"I'm not allowed to go rowing if my folks didn't give me permission."

"Man! You're really something." Herbie took a long swallow of soda. "You're going to stow away on a ship to Tokyo but you're chicken to ride around the lake in a rowboat."

"I'm not chicken!" But Herbie was absolutely right for once. What did she care if she didn't have permission to go rowing. What did it matter anymore! "Okay, let's go."

They ran to the dock at the lake, pooled all their money and rented a boat for half an hour. Glenn rowed first. Winnie and Tina sat in the back. Winnie leaned over the edge, letting her fingers skim the water. It felt good.

When they were out in the middle of the lake, Tina announced, "I have to make."

Glenn groaned. "Couldn't you have thought of that *before?*"

"I didn't have to before."

"Man! We're out in the middle of the lake Tina!" Herbie reminded her.

"What do you want me to do? Make in the boat?"

"You can hold it, can't you?" Winnie asked.

Tina covered her face with her hands and stood up. The boat rocked from side to side.

"For crying out loud, Tina! Sit down. I'll row in." Herbie changed places with Glenn and rowed in silently.

After Winnie took Tina to the ladies' room they decided to go home. They were out of money anyway and no one had brought a ball along. Somehow Tina and her complaints had spoiled the party mood. Herbie wasn't bad today, Winnie thought. Tina was impossible, but Herbie was okay. He even pulled the wagon home . . . without anybody asking him to. They stopped in front of Winnie's house.

"See you tomorrow," Herbie said.

"No, not tomorrow," Winnie told him. "Tomorrow, I've got to go shopping. I need new shoes for school."

"What do you need new school shoes for if you're going to Tokyo?" Herbie asked.

"Well, I need new shoes anyway. It doesn't matter for what. My old ones are a mess." Then she remembered about how she had asked them if their father looted stores to get shoes and her face reddened. But Herbie and Glenn laughed at her, and Winnie, feeling very foolish, laughed too.

"See you Tuesday then," Glenn said.

"I don't know about Tuesday. My brother's

coming home from camp and we're going into the city to meet his train."

"Oh. Well, okay. Thanks for the picnic." Herbie, Glenn and Tina started out for home.

"Hey, you guys!" Winnie called. "I'll see you on Wednesday, okay?"

That night, after dinner, Winnie and her parents settled down in the den, in front of the T.V. After a while, Mr. Barringer put down the sports magazine he was reading and said, "We thought you'd want to know we're not moving."

"We're not?" Winnie asked. She had been so sure her mother would get her own way.

"No. We decided this afternoon," her father said.

"Great!" Winnie jumped off the couch. "Then maybe we can have the Garbers over for dinner or something."

Mrs. Barringer put down the dress she was working on. It was Winnie's last year's plaid cotton and the hem had to be let down. "Now look Winnie . . . just because we aren't moving away right now doesn't mean that we're going to be best friends with the Garbers. After all, Iggie's family lived in that house for three years and Daddy and I never saw them socially."

"Oh." Winnie pushed her hair away from her face. "I thought you changed your mind."

Mrs. Barringer threaded her needle. "Changed my mind about what?"

"Well, we're not moving so I thought you changed your mind about . . . you know. . . ."

"Moving is just too much trouble," Mrs. Barringer sighed. She put the thread in her mouth and bit it off.

So, Winnie wouldn't be going to Tokyo after all! She was half disappointed. All those plans . . . down the drain. But if they weren't moving there wasn't any reason to run away! Winnie watched her mother sew the new hem. Then she looked at her father. He had fallen asleep in his chair. His mouth was half open and he was snoring. Winnie looked back at her mother . . . then back at her father . . . they didn't even notice.

They just don't care, Winnie thought. They don't care enough one way or the other . . . about *anything!* Too much trouble . . . that's what her mother said. It was *too much trouble!* They really took the easy way out.

Winnie got up without a word and went into the kitchen. She opened the refrigerator and grabbed a handful of cherries. She was careful not to slam the back door on her way outside.

She walked down the block, spitting cherry pits into the street. When she got to Iggie's house she hid in the shadow of the tall elm tree. The house looked cozy and inviting. But it really wasn't Iggie's house anymore. It belonged to the Garbers. Winnie remembered how Glenn said it the day they met. "This is the Garber house now."

She spit out her last cherry pit and turned away from the house. There was Woozie, wandering down the street, sniffing at trees. He wasn't supposed to be running around loose like that. Somebody might report him. "Here Woozie," Winnie called softly as she walked toward him. Woozie ran to her and licked her leg. Winnie bent down, resting her head against his soft fur. "Go on home now, Woozie. Go on . . . Glenn will be looking for you."

On Tuesday morning Winnie finished her letter to Iggie.

. . . And so the Landons are moving away but we're going to stay and so are the Garbers. Sunday night I stood in front of your house (I mean their house) for a long time and I guess I don't really know as much as I thought I did.
I miss you a lot!!!

Love,
Winnie

She licked the stamp and placed it upside down on the envelope. She wondered how long it would take to reach Tokyo. She jumped up onto her bed and studied her reflection in the dresser mirror. She threw her shoulders back and stood sideways. Still perfectly straight, but not *really* like a boy, she thought. She had given her mother the privilege of doing her hair. It wasn't every day that Matthew came home from camp. Winnie had to admit, her hair looked kind of nice. She smoothed out her dress and hopped off the bed.

"Winnie . . . are you ready? Daddy's in the car waiting," her mother called from downstairs.

"I'm coming . . . I'm coming," Winnie shouted back. She wondered how she would ever manage to tell Matthew everything that had happened this week. One week! Was that possible? It seemed like years. The Garbers should just see her now. They wouldn't even know her, all dressed up. Next week when school started she'd have to wear a dress every day. Yick!

Winnie spit the double wad of gum she was chewing into the waste basket and ran down the stairs.